The Phantom of Featherford Falls

Susan Sand, the famous mystery writer and detective, and her friend Marge Halloran, are expecting to spend a quiet holiday near the spectacular Featherford Falls. But the chilling appearance of a Phantom at the falls, and the suspicious behaviour of other guests at the Feather Inn mean another intriguing case for Susan to solve. But first she has to discover what can possibly be the connection between the ghost of a long-dead Indian warrior and a string of New York robberies.

Susan Sand Mystery Stories

SUSAN SAND

5

The Phantom of Featherford Falls

Marilyn Ezzell

Beaver Books

*To all the folks south of the Mason-Dixon line with love
from their northern cousin*

A Beaver Book
Published by Arrow Books Limited
17–21 Conway Street, London W1P 6JD
A division of the Hutchinson Publishing Group
London Melbourne Sydney Auckland Johannesburg
and agencies throughout the world

First published by
Pinnacle Books 1983
Beaver edition 1984
© Copyright text Marilyn Ezzell 1983

Set in Linoterm Baskerville
by JH Graphics Limited, Reading
Made and printed in Great Britain by
Anchor Brendon Limited, Tiptree, Essex

ISBN 0 09 936020 9

Contents

1

At the Feather Inn

'Susan, I'm here!' cried plump Marge Halloran as she climbed out of her car, clutching a large marmalade cat who squirmed desperately in an effort to jump to the ground.

'Marge, you're earlier than I expected!' replied Susan Sand, running down the steps of the Feather Inn, a smile on her pert face and her raven hair glistening in the bright summer sun. 'It's only ten-thirty!'

'There was almost no traffic,' explained Marge, panting somewhat and still firmly holding Susan's cat, Ikhnaton, who meowed loudly at the sight of his mistress. 'What a beautiful spot this is! Those mountains are breathtaking! Are the Featherford Falls far from here?'

'Only about a quarter of a mile,' replied Susan, reaching out her arms to take her pet, Icky.

At that moment an Indian boy of about fourteen, dressed in buckskin, appeared from around the corner of the historic rustic structure known as the Feather Inn. Trotting alongside him was an enormous dog, a beautiful creature who looked like a wolf.

'Here's Brave Deer, come to take your luggage,' said Susan, introducing the boy to Marge. 'And this is his dog, Wolf Dog. She really is half wolf!'

'A wolf!' screamed Marge. 'She's a real wolf! She's coming right for me! She's going to attack me!'

Indeed, Marge was right, for no sooner had Susan's red-haired friend turned to the Indian boy, Brave Deer, than Wolf Dog scented cat. Suddenly Icky sprang from Marge's arms. In one furry streak he fled across the broad expanse of lawn in front of the inn and up the trunk of an old oak on to a limb twenty feet from the ground. Wolf Dog, all her hunting instincts roused, barking shrilly, sped after the terrified cat, followed by Brave Deer and Susan. The Indian boy ran so swiftly, he reached the tree only a few seconds after his dog. Susan was astounded that anyone could run that fast, but at the moment all her thoughts were on Icky's safety.

Crouched on the limb, his back arched and his silky fur bristling, Ikhnaton hissed and spit, while Wolf Dog bounded at the bole of the huge oak, her barks causing a small party of people to emerge from the inn.

'Wolf Dog, down!' commanded the Indian boy in a low but stern voice. 'Go over there by the porch and sit!' Brave Deer pointed to a spot far from the tree, where a small veranda jutted out from the side of the inn.

Wolf Dog continued to bark and leap against the oak, but soon her master managed to gain control, for the animal was a well-trained and gentle creature whose only weakness was cats. Shortly after, she was sitting docilely in the shade by the porch, her huge pink tongue hanging out and an expression of guilt in her brown eyes.

'Miss Sand, I am very sorry that Wolf Dog behaved so badly,' said Brave Deer, his manner sombre and his tone sincere. 'She will not hurt your cat, for I will have a talk with her. She is very intelligent and will understand. It is only that she did not expect a cat to be a guest at the Feather Inn. Once she knows that Ikhnaton is to stay with you and your friend, she will not harm him.'

'I know Wolf Dog is a lovely dog,' replied Susan Sand. 'I should have told you that my friend was bringing my cat. The whole thing is my fault. But how are we going to get Icky down?'

'That will not be difficult,' replied the Indian boy. In no

time he had sprung to a low branch and then swung himself up to the limb where Icky crouched. Soon he was holding the cat in his strong brown arms. So fast had the Indian boy climbed the tree and so distracted was Icky by Wolf Dog sitting by the porch, that the cat was captured before he knew what had happened.

Several seconds later Brave Deer dropped to the ground and handed the frightened cat gently to Susan.

'Brave Deer, thank you,' replied Susan, clasping Icky to her. 'I never saw anyone climb a tree so quickly! You must take Marge and me to the Featherford Falls. I've heard how famous you are for your tours of the falls. People say that you are able to climb about like a deer on the slippery rocks.'

'I'm sorry, but that would be impossible,' replied Brave Deer in an abrupt manner which startled Susan, for the Indian boy had always been exceedingly polite. 'I no longer conduct people to the falls. Now I will take your friend's luggage to her room.'

Quickly Brave Deer turned and started for Marge's car. Susan looked after him, puzzled.

'Oh, Sue!' cried Marge, rushing up to her friend and laying her hands on Icky's head. 'Thank heavens Icky is all right! Imagine staying at an inn with a wolf!'

'Wolf Dog is only half wolf,' explained Susan again. 'The other half is police dog.'

'What difference does that make?' asked Marge, her freckles prominent on her flushed face. 'How can we stay here with that wild animal prowling around? I won't be able to sleep a wink!'

'Marge, Wolf Dog is no wild animal. Once she is used to Icky being here, there will be no danger. She is really a very nice dog. Brave Deer is going to have a talk with her. I'm certain from now on she will behave herself.'

'I wish I were as confident as you,' answered Marge. 'Isn't that Indian boy remarkable. He really does run like a deer.'

'Brave Deer is very famous in this area,' explained Susan, climbing the steps of the Feather Inn. 'His tours of the Featherford Falls attract a great deal of business for Mr Kingsley, the man who owns the inn. But something has happened. Brave Deer just told me that he no longer takes people to the falls. I wonder why?'

'I knew it! You've found another mystery,' teased Marge. 'I'm surprised it took you all this time. Why, you've been here for almost two weeks.'

Indeed, Susan Sand, the renowned author of mystery stories and an amateur sleuth, had just conducted a seminar on the art of the detective story. Every summer aspiring writers came to the Feather Inn to listen to famous authors like Susan. Her seminar was one of the most popular, and she had spent a busy, but stimulating, two weeks. People were intensely attracted by the nine-teen-year-old writer, for she had also become famous as a detective by solving a series of mysteries. During her first, the mystery at Hollowhearth House, she had been responsible for Marge Halloran's gaining possession of her rightful inheritance. Her last case, the riddle of Raggedrock Ridge, which had occurred the previous autumn, was still being written about in the newspapers.

As the friends walked up the steps and into the beautiful oak-beamed lobby of the inn, the small crowd of guests that had gathered began to disperse. Several smiled at the girls and made solicitous comments about Icky's welfare.

'What a beautiful cat, Miss Sand,' said a little blond man who stood behind the registration desk. He wore small steel-rimmed glasses and smiled broadly at Icky, who lay contentedly in Susan's arms. 'And this pretty redhead must be your friend, Miss Halloran. I am indeed sorry that we had to have such a disturbance upon your arrival. Wolf Dog is usually so well-behaved. I must have a talk with Brave Deer. We can't have his pet upsetting our guests.'

'Please don't be angry with Brave Deer, Mr Kingsley,'

Susan implored. 'He said he would talk to Wolf Dog and tell her not to harm Icky. I am certain nothing further will happen.'

'Thank you for taking such a tolerant view, Miss Sand,' replied Warren Kingsley. 'Brave Deer is a valuable employee of the inn, and he is very fond of that dog. If I made him get rid of the animal, I am positive that the boy would leave my employment.'

'Oh, don't insist on his giving Wolf Dog away!' Susan exclaimed. 'She is a lovely creature. Brave Deer would be heartbroken.'

Mr Kingsley smiled and nodded his head. 'Yes, yes, Miss Sand. You are right. The boy does love that dog. As long as she behaves herself, I will allow her to remain.'

'Mr Kingsley, Brave Deer tells me that he no longer takes people on tours of the Featherford Falls,' Susan said, adjusting her glasses. 'He seemed very adamant about it. Has something happened to cause him to stop the tours?'

Mr Kingsley turned and went back behind the registration desk. 'He is a strange boy, Miss Sand,' he replied, pushing a big book towards the edge of the desk. 'He says very little. The tours were an important attraction here at the inn. But if the boy does not want to conduct them any longer, I cannot force him to. Miss Halloran, will you please sign your name in the ledger.'

Mr Kingsley smiled at Marge as she took up the pen and signed her name. 'Your room is right next to Miss Sand's,' he announced. 'It is one of our most pleasant ones. I hope you will be very comfortable, and if there is anything you need, please don't hesitate to ask me or my daughter.'

He pushed a bell on the desk. In almost no time a pale girl of about twelve, tall for her age, emerged through a door behind the counter.

'You wanted me, Father?' she asked quietly, her hands folded in front of her.

'Yes, Claudia. This is Miss Marge Halloran, Miss

Sand's friend. Please take her to her room and make certain she has everything she needs.'

'Yes, Father,' the girl replied. 'This way, Miss Halloran. Has Brave Deer taken your luggage?'

'Yes, Claudia,' Marge replied. 'He brought it up a short while ago.'

The two friends followed Claudia Kingsley up the winding staircase to the third floor, down a long, well-carpeted hall to a door at the end of the corridor.

'Here is your room, Miss Halloran,' Claudia said, opening the door and ushering the girls inside. 'I hope you will like it.'

'Oh, it's lovely!' Marge exclaimed, rushing to the window. 'And the view is wonderful!'

'I'm right next door,' Susan said. 'There's a communicating door, so it's almost as if we had the same room.'

Susan put Icky on the floor, and he immediately began an intensive investigation, warily looking about him.

'He is making certain that Wolf Dog is not around,' said Susan, laughing.

'Oh, I am so sorry about that!' Claudia Kingsley exclaimed. 'Please don't hold it against Brave Deer. I know he feels terrible.' She twisted her hands nervously and looked imploringly at Susan Sand.

'Please don't be upset,' Susan said consolingly. 'Nothing happened to Ikhnaton.'

'I'm so glad he is all right,' Claudia replied. 'And now I must get back to work. Please call me, Miss Halloran, if there is anything you need.'

'Thank you, Claudia,' Marge answered. 'Perhaps you would like to go on a picnic with us during my stay here?'

'Oh, thank you, but that would be impossible,' the girl replied, looking down at the floor. 'My father never allows me to leave the inn this time of year. We are so busy.'

'But surely he can spare you for one day,' Marge insisted. 'Why don't you ask him?'

12

'Thank you, Miss Halloran,' Claudia said again. 'But I don't think he would agree. Now I must go.'

Claudia smiled shyly and left the room, closing the door quietly behind her.

'Why, the poor girl!' Marge exclaimed.

'Her father must be very strict with her,' Susan said. 'She needs to get out in the sun. She is so pale. Perhaps if we talk to Mr Kingsley he will let her go swimming with us.'

'I think Mr Kingsley is mean to be so severe with her,' said Marge vehemently.

At that moment there was a knock on the door. Susan quickly opened it. Brave Deer stood erect on the threshold, Wolf Dog sitting obediently at his side.

'Wolf Dog has come to apologise,' the Indian boy said, his face stern.

Wolf Dog looked up at Susan, a contrite expression in her gentle brown eyes, and held up her right paw.

'Oh, Wolf Dog, how clever you are!' Susan said, taking the large foot in her hand. 'I accept your apology and I know you will never run after Ikhnaton again.'

Icky, his back arched, sidled sideways along the wall of the room, spitting. Wolf Dog remained placidly sitting, her paw in Susan's hand.

'Icky, you must learn to be friends. Wolf Dog is not going to harm you,' urged Susan.

'We must go now,' said Brave Deer. 'I have work to do. Come, Wolf Dog!'

The Indian boy bowed quickly and retreated down the hall, his pet walking slowly by his side.

'What a remarkable boy,' said Susan, closing the door. 'I would like to get to know him better.'

'Claudia Kingsley is very fond of him,' replied Marge, smiling.

Once Marge had unpacked and settled into her room, she and Susan decided to go for a drive. Because the day was hot, they brought their swimsuits and spent several hours splashing about in a beautiful natural pool not far from the inn. After returning to the inn for dinner, the girls set out again for a drive in the moonlight, leaving Icky to prowl about the hotel, nocturnal investigation being one of his favourite pastimes.

The hour was well past midnight before the girls returned and crept silently up the stairs to their third-floor rooms. No one was about except for a clerk at the desk in the lobby.

'What a spooky place this is at night!' whispered Marge. 'I wish we had a torch. These nightlights don't give much light.'

'My torch is in my car,' returned Susan in a low voice, as the friends reached the third floor. Suddenly Susan stopped and gripped Marge's arm. 'Look! Over near my door! Who is that man, and what is he doing to Icky?'

'I can hardly see anything,' replied Marge, her voice tense. 'He seems to be grabbing at Icky's front paw! Oh, Sue, do you think he is trying to harm him?'

'No,' Susan replied, her detective instincts on the alert. 'He seems to be examining Icky's paw. Let's watch for a moment.'

'Why on earth would he want to do that in the middle of the night?' Marge asked. 'He must be crazy!'

The scene was indeed a peculiar one, for the man was crouched in front of Icky, both of his large hands holding the cat's right front paw, while Icky desperately tried to free himself.

'He appears to be picking at the fur between Icky's toes,' said Susan, leaning forward and straining to see in the dim light. 'He's very intent on what he is doing.'

Suddenly Susan's anger came to the fore, and she rushed from her hiding place. 'Sir, I demand to know who you are and what you are doing to my cat!' she cried.

2

Detective work

Instantly the man dropped Icky's paw and whirled about. He was tall and powerfully built, and as he stood and faced the girls, Susan gasped.

'Mr Hearne!' she exclaimed. 'Barry Hearne!'

'Miss Sand, I – I – I suppose you wonder what I was doing,' he replied sheepishly, stepping forward awkwardly.

'Yes, Mr Hearne, we are extremely curious,' returned Susan, adjusting her glasses. 'This is my friend, Marge Halloran. Marge, this is Barry Hearne. He was a member of my seminar. What were you doing, Mr Hearne?'

'Well, you see, Miss Sand,' the man began haltingly, 'I was walking down the hall and I saw this cat – I had no idea he was your cat – sort of limping and picking up his foot and shaking it, so, being an animal-lover, I had to see what was wrong.'

'And what did you discover?' Susan asked, sweeping Icky into her arms and examining his right front paw.

'Well, I could see that something is stuck in the fur between his toes,' Barry Hearne replied. 'But then you came along and surprised me.'

'Yes, there is a piece of something sticking to the fur,' Susan said, intently studying her pet's foot. 'I'll take him back to my room and remove it. Thank you, Mr Hearne, for taking such an interest in Icky. I worry about him. He seems to be fond of getting into trouble.'

'I'm glad that he isn't hurt,' Barry Hearne replied, smiling genially. 'Now I think I will be off to bed. It's nice to have met you, Miss Halloran.'

Barry Hearne reached out his big hand and vigorously shook hands with both Susan and Marge. Then he turned and sauntered down the hall towards the stairs.

'What was that all about?' whispered Marge, stroking Icky's silky head.

'Let's go into my room,' Susan answered, turning towards the door. 'I want to get a better look at Icky's paw.'

Once inside Susan's room, the girls sat down on the bed. By the bright light of the bedside lamp they examined the cat's paw.

'It's wax,' Susan discovered. 'It is unquestionably wax. I'll have to cut it out with my sewing scissors.'

'Where would Icky pick up a piece of wax?' Marge asked. 'And why was Barry Hearne so interested in it?'

'It's very curious,' Susan said quietly. 'I find Mr Hearne a very nice person, but I can't imagine why he wants to become a writer. He has no talent whatsoever, yet he faithfully attended all my classes and worked very hard on his assignments.'

'He doesn't seem like the writer type,' Marge mused. 'And why would he be creeping around the halls at this hour?'

'You don't really believe Mr Hearne's explanation, do you, Marge?' Susan replied.

'Well, he was acting rather oddly, wasn't he, Sue?' the redhead answered.

'Yes, I agree with you,' Susan said. 'He could have been returning from a date, which would explain why he was up and dressed, but his actions are suspicious. His room is on the second floor, and he was upset that we saw him.'

'But what possible interest could Mr Hearne have in a piece of wax stuck in a cat's paw?' Marge asked again.

'There must be something significant about the wax,' Susan responded, snipping off the tuft of fur with the sticky stuff attached to it. 'This must have been soft when Icky stepped in it,' she said, holding up the piece. 'It's almost hard now. Icky, where did you step in this?'

Ikhnaton, Amenhotep IV, named after the Egyptian pharaoh, rubbed himself against his mistress and purred loudly.

'Oh, Icky, if only you could talk,' said Susan Sand, kissing her pet on the head.

'I can see that he is not going to tell us,' Marge retorted, yawning. 'I am going to bed. I went swimming today. No wonder I'm so tired. It's after one o'clock!'

'You go to bed if you want to,' Susan replied. 'I am going to investigate. Perhaps I can find out where Icky picked up this wax.'

'Then you do think it's important,' Marge said.

'Yes, I do.'

'And you can't resist investigating.'

Susan Sand laughed and jumped to her feet. 'You go to bed, sleepyhead,' she teased. 'I'm going to my car to get my torch.'

'You're not leaving me out of a mystery!' Marge replied. 'Where do we start?'

'We'll comb every inch of the halls,' Susan said as the girls left the room and walked down the silent corridor.

Susan ran quickly to her car and returned several minutes later with her torch. Methodically, the girls began a minute investigation of the third-floor hall.

'I told the man at the desk that I lost my pen,' Susan explained. 'Otherwise he might become too curious. The third floor is the best place to start, since this is where we found Icky and Barry Hearne.'

'But Icky could have picked up that piece of wax any-where in the building, or even outside,' Marge returned. 'It seems like an impossible task, Sue. You know Icky. He goes everywhere.'

'You are right, Marge,' Susan agreed. 'Most likely we will find nothing. But I doubt that Icky was outside. He had no earth on his feet, and he hasn't washed them since he stepped in the wax. Perhaps he will be lucky and find another bit of the stuff. At least it's worth a try.'

Quietly the girls searched every inch of the third-floor hall, Susan shining her light into every crack and corner. Three times they walked up one side of the hall and back down the other. Nothing was discovered.

'We'll work our way down the stairs,' said Susan.

'Why downstairs instead of up?' Marge asked.

'It's just a hunch,' Susan replied. 'Barry Hearne's room is on the second floor.'

Silently the girls continued their search. The halls were dark and empty. Downstairs in the lobby the grandfather clock chimed twice and continued its incessant ticking. Susan Sand slowly flashed her light back and forth, peering through her glasses, now and then stopping to look more closely at the floor. Suddenly, about a third of the way down the hall, she stopped and picked up something.

'We're in luck!' she exclaimed softly in Marge's ear, her green eyes sparkling. 'This is wax!'

'Oh, Sue, how exciting!' Marge squealed.

'Sssh!' warned Susan, gripping her friend's hand. 'We don't want to be heard. Let's get back upstairs and talk this over.'

'Where is Barry Hearne's room?' whispered Marge, unable to contain her enthusiasm.

Susan Sand pointed down the hall to a door at the end of the corridor and pulled Marge along towards the stairs. Just as the girls reached the first step, Susan stopped and turned her head.

'What is it, Sue?' Marge asked, her eyes widening.

'Someone saw us,' she whispered, straining to see in the dim light. 'I know I heard a door close.'

18

'Which door, Sue?' Marge asked, looking over her friend's shoulder.

'I don't know,' Susan Sand answered, attempting to suppress her excitement. 'If only I had been a second sooner! Someone was spying on us, Marge. Who could it have been?'

3

A deepening mystery

'Barry Hearne! It must have been Barry Hearne!' said Marge excitedly.

'He's the most likely possibility,' agreed Susan Sand, peering down the dark hall. 'But there is no way of knowing for certain. If only I had turned my head a moment sooner!'

The girls returned to Susan's room and looked at each other.

'What does it mean, Sue?' asked Marge. 'I'm beginning to get a spooky feeling, and I can't explain why. Maybe Barry Hearne was telling the truth when he said he just wanted to help Icky because he was limping.'

'That's possible but most unlikely,' returned Susan, holding up the small piece of wax she had found on the second floor. 'Barry Hearne was interested in the wax on Icky's paw. Now why should he be prowling around the halls after midnight, fully dressed? He wasn't even on his own floor.'

'Someone is certainly curious,' said Marge. 'Curious enough to be up and peeking through their door at two a.m. If that person wasn't Barry Hearne, then who was it?'

'We have found another mystery, Marge,' replied Susan Sand, smiling mischievously.

'And I thought I was going to have a restful holiday!' Marge retorted. 'If I don't get some sleep, I'm going to fall over!'

'You go to bed,' said Susan. 'How I wish Icky could tell us where he got that wax. Was he on the second floor, where we found this, or was he somewhere else in the hotel?'

'You can sit up for what remains of the night and think about it,' replied Marge, yawning. 'I am going to get some sleep.'

As Marge walked wearily towards the door to her room, she passed the windows that looked out on the broad, moonlit expanse of lawn in front of the Feather Inn. Suddenly she gave out a loud squeal.

'Sue! Look!' she cried, pointing out one of the windows. 'There's someone running from the inn – an Indian. He's running like the wind, right into the woods.'

Susan Sand rushed over to the window and looked out.

'That's Black Cloud!' Susan exclaimed. 'I would know him anywhere, Marge. He's Brave Deer's uncle and a famous woodsman. He takes people on camping trips into the woods, often for a week at a time. But why is he here, and at this hour? Only this morning he left with a party of campers from the inn.'

'Black Cloud?' asked Marge. 'I think I have heard of him from one of the boys at Irongate University who is keen on camping. I believe he went on one of Black Cloud's trips.'

'Black Cloud lives in a log cabin in the woods,' Susan explained, 'but the cabin is not in the direction in which he is running.'

'He's gone,' said Marge. 'I would never have seen him if the moon wasn't so bright.'

'One mystery on top of another,' mused Susan Sand. 'What is Black Cloud doing here when he should be miles away with his camping party?'

'I doubt if he wanted anyone to see him,' Marge surmised. 'Only by chance did I happen to look out the window.'

'Black Cloud is a respected person,' said Susan, leaning

against the window frame and wrinkling her forehead. 'He is taciturn and aloof, but his integrity is beyond question. Brave Deer is proud of him and tries to emulate him. What brought Black Cloud to the inn, and why did he run off as if he didn't want to be seen?'

'And in the opposite direction from his cabin?' added Marge.

'He must be heading back to the camping party,' Susan deduced, crossing the room and sitting down on the edge of the bed, where Icky was curled in blissful sleep.

'Which means that he left the group in the woods and ran all the way to the Feather Inn in the middle of the night,' responded Marge. 'Why would he want to do that?'

'It's peculiar,' pondered Susan, removing her glasses and staring into space. 'And on the very night when Barry Hearne is prowling about the inn.'

'Perhaps there is a connection,' offered Marge.

'I can't imagine what it could be,' replied Susan, 'but it certainly is mysterious.'

'Now I really am going to bed,' said Marge, 'before a whole party of Indians arrives and carries me off into the woods.'

'I'm rather sleepy myself.' laughed Susan, starting to undress. 'Tomorrow morning we'll be able to think about this with clear heads.'

The following morning Susan and Marge were up and dressed before nine o'clock.

'For some reason I didn't want to sleep any longer,' said Marge as the girls descended the stairs on their way to the dining-room for breakfast. 'This country air makes me want to rise and shine!'

'And solve mysteries,' retorted Susan Sand.

At that moment a door on the second floor opened, and a small, plump man with a black case over one shoulder emerged and greeted Susan enthusiastically. He was accompanied by a little fat woman carrying a camera, who beamed warmly at the girls.

'Well, Miss Susan Sand,' said the little man. 'Good morning. Mrs Tanner and I are off on another hunt. Such a beautiful day!'

'Good morning, Mr Tanner, Mrs Tanner,' replied Susan. 'This is my friend, Marge Halloran. The Tanners are botanists, Marge. In fact, they have written two books on wild flowers.'

'How interesting,' said Marge, shaking hands with the pair. 'My mother and I run a bookshop in the town of Thornewood. We have one of your books in stock right now. I have looked through it. The photographs are beautiful!'

'All due to my wife,' replied Mr Tanner. 'She is an expert photographer. I would be lost without her.'

'And what are you girls planning to do on such a lovely day?' asked Mrs Tanner pleasantly.

'We will probably go to the Featherford Falls,' returned Susan. 'Marge has never seen them.'

'A wonderful sight,' Mrs Tanner said. 'Quite breathtaking, in fact. I have taken several pictures of the falls.'

Once in the dining-room, the girls bade good day to the Tanners and seated themselves near a large window that looked out on lush green mountains and valleys.

'We are very high up,' said Marge. 'What a pleasant place to eat breakfast!'

'Icky is dining in the kitchen on fresh fish caught yesterday,' said Susan. 'Mr Kingsley called me on the house phone earlier to tell me so.'

'Lucky Icky!' replied Marge. 'He always gets the best out of everything. Oh! Who is that impressive-looking woman?'

A tall grey-haired woman dressed in hiking clothes had just entered the dining-room. Although her clothes were not elegant, she had a distinguished bearing and an authoritative manner of speaking.

'Good morning, Mrs Vandervelden,' said Mr Kingsley as he seated her at a table near the girls. 'I understand you arrived late last night.'

'Just after midnight, Warren,' she answered. 'Delighted to be here. In fact, sometimes I think that I could spend my life here! The air is so invigorating, and I'm impatient to get off on another camping trip with Black Cloud.'

'Oh, dear,' replied the owner of the Feather Inn. 'A whole party left just yesterday morning. If only I had known you were coming, they would have waited for you.'

'Oh, what a shame!' replied Mrs Vandervelden. 'I got my dates wrong. Well, I will just have to wait for the next trek.'

Mr Kingsley left the woman to order her breakfast and came over to Susan and Marge.

'Good morning, Mrs Kingsley,' said Susan. 'Who is that distinguished-looking woman? Her name sounds familiar.'

'Mrs Vandervelden is a very wealthy woman from an old New York family,' said Mr Kingsley proudly. 'She is a keen camper and comes to the inn at least three times a year. Most of the time she lives in her town house in New York.'

'Warren, I hear you talking about me,' said Mrs Vandervelden, rising from her chair and crossing over to the girls' table. 'I have to meet this young lady. You are Susan Sand, if I am not mistaken. I have seen your picture in the paper – but you are even more striking in person.'

'Thank you,' Susan replied graciously. 'Why don't you join us for breakfast? This is my friend, Marge Halloran.'

'Delighted!' Mrs Vandervelden responded, seating herself. 'I am a fan of yours, Miss Sand. I just love your books, especially the last one, *The Invisible Mirror*. But *The Bony Finger* was excellent, too.'

'You are very kind,' said Susan, smiling. 'I am always happy to meet my fans.'

'And what are you girls going to do on this lovely day?'

Mrs Vandervelden asked. 'I thought that since— Why, there's Brave Deer and Wolf Dog. Good morning!'

The Indian boy and his dog had just entered the dining-room through a side door that led to the patio. Hearing Mrs Vandervelden's voice, Brave Deer waved and came over to the table.

'Mrs Vandervelden, I am glad to see you again,' the boy said politely. 'It is too bad that my uncle left yesterday. You will have to wait a week for another trip.'

'Can't be helped,' the woman replied in her forthright manner. 'And how have you been? And Claudia? And you, Wolf Dog?' She reached out her hand and patted the big animal on the head.

'We are fine, thank you,' Brave Deer replied. 'Claudia is waiting in the restaurant this morning. She is over by the kitchen.'

'Good, good. I am anxious to see her. Since I missed Black Cloud's trip, perhaps you could take me and Claudia and these girls, if they wish, to the Featherford Falls. We could make a day of it.'

'Mrs Vandervelden – I – it would be impossible for me to take you to the falls. Absolutely impossible. You see—'

Brave Deer's usually controlled manner changed so suddenly that Susan wondered what was the matter with him. He had become so agitated that he was barely able to talk.

'Brave Deer, what is wrong?' Mrs Vandervelden asked in a kindly voice, taking the boy's hand.

'I can't take you to the falls, Mrs Vandervelden,' he almost shouted. Then he wrenched his hand from the woman's grasp and rushed from the dining-room, Wolf Dog close on his heels.

At that moment there was a loud crash from the area near the kitchen.

'What is wrong with Claudia?' Mrs Vandervelden cried, rising from her chair. 'She has dropped a whole tray of dishes. Oh, I am afraid she is going to faint!'

25

4

The Featherford Falls

Mrs Vandervelden, Susan, and Marge rushed over to Claudia Kingsley, who stood swaying and holding on to the kitchen door. Her face was ashen, and in her brown eyes was an expression of apprehension.

'What is the matter, Claudia?' Mrs Vandervelden said, placing a supporting arm around the girl's slim form and helping her to a nearby seat, which Susan had placed for her.

'It's nothing,' the girl said faintly, holding her head and leaning forward. 'The kitchen is very hot. Suddenly I became dizzy, but it's passing off now.'

'You need to rest,' Susan suggested, kneeling down by Claudia's chair. 'It's a lovely day. Why don't you come on a picnic with us?'

'Oh, I couldn't do that,' Claudia replied, looking earnestly at Susan and Marge. 'You are very nice to ask me, but my father needs me here in the dining-room. The inn is very full at the moment.'

Mr Kingsley had entered the room and, seeing his daughter seated in a chair and a group of people around her, hurried over.

'Claudia, what is wrong?' he asked in a low voice. 'You've lost all your colour.'

'I'm all right, Father,' the girl replied meekly. 'I just had a fainting spell.'

'A fainting spell? That doesn't sound like you.'

'The kitchen is very hot,' Claudia explained. 'I'm certain that's what caused it.'

'Perhaps she should take the day off,' Susan said tactfully. 'Marge and I and Mrs Vandervelden were just discussing what we should do. I think a trip to the falls would be good for Claudia.'

'Well, now, that is very kind of you, Susan,' Warren Kingsley answered. 'But today I can't do without her. And, by the way, where is Brave Deer? I need him at the desk.'

'He was just here,' Mrs Vandervelden said. 'I was talking to him only a moment before Claudia had her fainting spell. Claudia, you do need a rest. You really should go with us to the falls.'

'Oh, no, Mrs Vandervelden,' the blonde girl replied. 'Father needs me here. I was silly to feel faint. I'm fine now. Please, let me get back to the kitchen.'

Claudia rose quickly from her chair and, thanking Susan, Marge, and Mrs Vandervelden for their concern, retreated through the kitchen door.

'Really, Warren, how can you let that girl work when she is obviously not well?' Mrs Vandervelden said in a stern voice.

'She has a mind of her own,' Mr Kingsley retorted in a somewhat nettled manner. 'I must get back to the desk. We are expecting new arrivals any moment. Thank you for asking Claudia on a picnic. Perhaps she will be able to go at another time.

'Mrs Vandervelden, you seem to know the Kingsleys quite well,' said Susan after they had returned to their table. 'Can you think of any reason why Claudia should look so disturbed?'

'No, Susan, I can't,' the woman replied. 'But I, too, saw the expression on Claudia's face.'

'And what is troubling Brave Deer?' asked Marge. 'He is very upset. Why doesn't he want to take you to the falls?'

'Strange! Very strange!' Mrs Vandervelden said in a whisper. 'There is something serious bothering those two young people, and I intend to find out what it is! If you girls will just excuse me, I am going to find Brave Deer and have a talk with him.'

Mrs Vandervelden rose from her seat and hurried from the dining-room, while Susan and Marge continued with their breakfast. Within a short time the older woman returned and seated herself once more at the table.

'Well, that's settled for the moment,' Mrs Vandervelden said decisively. 'Brave Deer has consented to take us to the falls. Girls, I think there is a romance going on between those two young people.'

'I suspected Claudia was very fond of Brave Deer,' Marge said.

'Yet there is more to this than romance, isn't there, Mrs Vandervelden?' said Susan.

'Possibly there is, Susan,' the woman replied non-committally. 'I didn't want to press Brave Deer. Now I think we should be off to the falls. I'll have a picnic lunch prepared. Make certain you wear thick clothes and rubber-soled shoes. We go behind the falls, you know, right into the big cave. It's somewhat dangerous, but the falling water is breathtaking.'

'How exciting!' cried Marge. 'I'm going up to my room to change.'

Within an hour Susan, Marge, Mrs Vandervelden, Brave Deer, and Wolf Dog started out for the Featherford Falls. Susan considered taking Icky, but decided that her pet would be much happier roaming about the Inn.

'Wolf Dog and Icky on a picnic!' Marge exclaimed. 'We'd spend the whole day keeping them apart.'

'Wolf Dog is very well behaved,' Brave Deer replied. 'She will not harm your cat, Miss Sand.'

'I know she won't, Brave Deer,' Susan replied.

'I was only teasing,' added Marge, noticing the boy's sober expression. 'Wolf Dog and I have actually become friends.'

Brave Deer smiled briefly and seemed somewhat mollified as he led the group along a narrow dirt road that

28

skirted Feather Creek. He was dressed in buckskin and wearing moccasins. The day was sunny and already hot. After about half a mile's walk, the booming sound of the falls could be heard in the distance. Soon the ground began to rise, and ahead through the thick trees a glimpse of sparkling water could be seen.

'Look! The Featherford Falls!' cried Marge, pointing. 'I can see the falling water!'

Suddenly the woods thinned out and the group looked up in awe at the grandeur of the falling water rushing down from a great height and splashing into a swirling pool at the base of the cliff.

'It's beautiful!' said Susan. 'I can feel the spray already.'

'Wait until we go inside and look through the water,' Mrs Vandervelden replied. 'That is one of the most splendid sights I have ever seen.'

The party chose a spot near the falls, yet out of range of the spray, to spread out their blanket. Not far away was a wet, rocky path that led up the side of the cliff, and another path that entered the cave. As Brave Deer stood looking up at the awesome sight, Susan noticed a reverent expression on the boy's face.

'We don't feel the way he does,' Susan said to herself. 'I know we don't. He seems to feel a special affinity with this spot. Most likely his ancestors lived around here. This is his territory.'

'It is indeed beautiful, Brave Deer,' said Susan quietly to the Indian boy.

'It is not only the beauty,' Brave Deer responded, a slight smile crossing his lips. 'It is the spirit that is in the water and in the rocks. You can feel it, can you not, Miss Sand?'

'Yes,' Susan replied, 'but not the way you do, Brave Deer. Perhaps if I lived here for a long time, I would be able to feel like you.'

'You are very keen, Miss Sand,' Brave Deer said,

29

looking at the black-haired girl standing next to him. 'Most people do not understand how we Indians respond to nature. This is my favourite place, I come here all the time, as did my ancestors.'

'You prefer to come alone,' Susan said.

'Yes,' the boy admitted, 'but I also enjoy taking groups into the cave.'

'Oh, let's go inside right now!' squealed Marge.

Brave Deer, with Wolf Dog at his side, led the way along the slippery, rocky path, around a jutting boulder, and into the big, damp cave just behind the falling water.

'Take small steps and do not try to hurry,' Brave Deer advised. 'Follow me, and you will not slip.'

Carefully Susan, Marge, and Mrs Vandervelden, who was somewhat behind, followed the Indian boy along the path. Once inside the cave, Susan and Marge stopped and looked out through the falling water.

'Oh!' exclaimed Marge, 'I can see all the colours of the rainbow! The water shimmers like glass!'

Suddenly she called out and pointed to her right, towards the woods on the other side of the falls. 'Who is that?' she cried. 'That Indian boy? He's dressed like you, Brave Deer, but he is younger.'

Through the falling water a figure could be seen moving about on the edge of the woods. The sight was eerie because the shimmering water lent an unreal appearance to the scene. The figure swayed back and forth for several seconds and then seemed to come closer. Without warning Brave Deer gave out a loud shriek and turned and ran wildly from the cave. Wolf Dog growled and snarled and followed the boy along the path.

'Brave Deer, what is wrong?' Susan called after the Indian.

Mrs Vandervelden, who had been some distance behind the group, turned and followed him as he ran past her.

30

'Brave Deer!' Susan called again, starting to run after the pair.

'Susan, let me talk to the boy alone,' Mrs Vandervelden pleaded when she saw the girl behind her. 'I'm the one who got him to come, so I feel responsible.'

Susan nodded her head in understanding and turned about. 'Marge,' she began. 'What could be— Marge, where are you?'

Susan called out again for her friend, but Marge had disappeared! Nor was there any evidence of the Indian child who had caused Brave Deer to run in such terror.

'Marge!' Susan cried.

Noticing that another rocky path led from the cave in the direction that the figure had been seen, Susan carefully picked her way over the stones and soon emerged from the cave on the other side from where the party had entered.

'Marge!' Susan repeated, but there was no response.

Alongside the falls was a narrow dirt track, and Susan decided to follow it. Walking up the steep incline, she looked around for any sign of Marge Halloran, but the area was completely deserted. Several times she knelt down, hoping to find a footprint or some other clue. At last she spotted an area where the dirt had been disturbed, just in front of a huge boulder. Rushing over to the site, Susan bent down and saw fresh footprints. Hurrying around the rock, Susan cried out in alarm, for there was Marge, lying on the ground.

'Marge!' Susan cried frantically. 'Oh, Marge, what has happened to you?'

5

The Phantom of the Falls

'Marge!' Susan cried again as she rushed over to her friend and knelt down by her prostrate form.

'Sue?' murmured the redhead in a weak voice. She opened her eyes and looked up into Susan's anxious face.

'Marge, what happened?' Susan asked, placing her arm under Marge's head and helping her to a sitting position.

'Oh, my head!' said Marge, placing a hand on the base of her skull. 'I was following the Indian boy when someone came up behind me and hit me on the head.'

'You mean someone knocked you out?'

'And how!' Marge exclaimed, scrambling to her feet. 'I must have seen the entire universe in just a few seconds.'

'I must get you back to the inn,' Susan said, holding her friend's arm firmly.

'Oh, no, Sue,' Marge answered. 'I'll be all right in a few minutes. We still have our picnic lunch to eat, and now we have another mystery to solve.'

'Why did you follow that boy?' Susan asked.

'Because I was convinced that the "boy" was Claudia,' Marge retorted.

'Claudia!' Susan exclaimed. 'What ever made you think that?'

'Sue, there was something about the way she moved that made me instinctively think that the figure was Claudia,' Marge said. 'I was so certain that I decided to confront her. As soon as she saw me coming, she turned and started up the path, running very fast, and I had a

32

hard time keeping up. When I got to this boulder, I felt a terrific pain in the back of my head, and then everything went blank. Whoever hit me must have dragged me behind the boulder.'

'How extraordinary!' Susan exclaimed as she helped Marge back towards the picnic site. 'And you heard no one behind you?'

'Not a sound. I was so intent on catching up with the "boy", I never thought of anyone else being around. The area seemed so deserted.'

'Marge, if you are right and that Indian boy really is Claudia, we've got some real investigating to do,' Susan stated, her green eyes shining. 'What possible reason could Claudia Kingsley have for dressing up as a twelve-year-old Indian boy and playing around in front of the falls?'

'And why should Brave Deer become so terrified?' Marge added. 'I didn't see anything frightening about that figure.'

'But Brave Deer did,' Susan said decisively. 'He is anything but a coward, yet the sight of that Indian boy moving about through the falling water caused him to run away in panic.'

'It makes no sense at all,' Marge responded, still rubbing her head.

'Oh, look, Marge,' cried Susan, running to a spot just off the path and bending over. 'There is a big black feather lying here on the ground.'

'I think there was a black feather in the headband of that Indian "boy",' replied Marge.

'It must have fallen out when he was running up the path,' Susan deduced, holding up the piece of plumage. 'I think I will keep this as a clue.'

Susan placed the feather in her pocket, and the pair continued on towards the picnic site. In order to return to the area where the group had laid out the blanket, it was necessary to go back into the cave behind the falls and over the rocky path that led to the other side. The only other route was to walk along the Feather Creek to a footbridge that spanned the water, but the small bridge was quite a distance away.

Just as the friends were about to enter the cave, Susan stopped and grasped Marge's arm. 'Marge, look over there by that tree,' she said in a low voice. 'Isn't that Barry Hearne?'

'Yes, it is,' Marge agreed. 'What is he doing here?'

'I can't imagine,' replied Susan. 'Come let's talk to him. He's seen us and he's waving.'

'Hello, Miss Sand, Miss Halloran,' the big man called out in a hearty manner, coming towards them. 'What are you two doing on this side of the falls?'

'We might ask you the same question,' said Susan, smiling.

'I see that you are about to enter the cave,' he answered, grinning broadly and seeming very much at ease. 'Quite a sight from inside, isn't it?'

'Then you've been in the cave and looked out through the falling water?' Marge asked.

'Oh, yes, several times,' the man replied. 'Brave Deer took me last week – but, you know, a strange thing just happened.' Barry Hearne lowered his voice and came closer to the pair. 'A short time ago, when I reached the bridge to cross the creek, I ran into Brave Deer and Mrs Vandervelden coming along the road. The boy was obviously quite upset, and Mrs Vandervelden was talking to him in her motherly manner. Just as I passed them, I heard Brave Deer say something about "the Phantom of the Falls". Now what do you think he could have meant by that?'

'The Phantom of the Falls?' repeated Marge. 'Oh, Sue—'

'I can't imagine what Brave Deer could have been talking about,' Susan interrupted, her hand closing over Marge's arm. 'Indians have a lot of folklore, Mr Hearne, which we know nothing about.'

'That's true, Miss Sand,' the man agreed. 'But I thought perhaps you would know what he meant, since you had all gone on a picnic together.'

'Oh, you knew we were coming to the falls?' Susan asked.

'You can't go very far around here without people knowing what you are doing,' Barry Hearne replied, flashing his good-natured smile.

'And what are you doing on this side of the creek?' Susan asked boldly.

'I love this spot,' the man replied. 'It's almost always deserted, and I can think about my writing without being interrupted.'

'How is your writing coming along?' Susan asked.

'Not so good,' Barry Hearne said, laughing. 'I don't think you have a very high opinion of my talent, Miss Sand.'

Susan Sand adjusted her glasses and looked up at the big man. 'Just why did you take my course, Mr Hearne?' she asked.

'To learn how to write, like everyone else,' he answered. 'Are you trying to tell me I'm wasting my time?'

'No, Mr Hearne. I wouldn't discourage anyone from doing what they want to do.'

'You're quite a girl,' Barry Hearne said, his face assuming a serious expression. 'You've got a lot of brains in that pretty head.'

'Thank you, Mr Hearne,' Susan replied. 'I'll consider that a compliment.'

'And you don't know who "the Phantom of the Falls" is?'

'I never heard the term before,' Susan answered truthfully. 'Would you care to join us on our picnic?'

'That's very kind of you, Susan, but I'm going to walk farther into the woods and do some thinking. It's been nice talking to you. Goodbye for now. I'll see you later, back at the inn.'

'Susan,' began Marge when Barry Hearne was out of earshot, 'do you think he could be the one who hit me over the head?'

'He was right in this area,' Susan said. 'But what possible reason could he have for doing such a thing?'

'What does Brave Deer mean by "the Phantom of the Falls"?'

'He must believe that the "boy" he saw through the falling water was a phantom,' Susan reasoned.

'But that's ridiculous!' Marge exclaimed. 'I know that the "boy" was Claudia Kingsley.'

'Brave Deer apparently thinks there is a phantom that haunts the falls,' Susan replied.

'He seems like such a sensible boy,' Marge stated.

'We mustn't come to any hasty conclusions,' Susan warned. 'We don't yet know the truth. Marge, are you absolutely convinced that that Indian figure was Claudia?'

'As positive as I could be under the circumstances,' Marge replied. 'Naturally, in that buckskin outfit and with straight black hair that must have been a wig, she looked exactly like a boy, but I was very close to her. For a moment I thought she realised that I knew who she was. Oh, Sue, it's hard to explain how one knows something. I just *felt* that the person was Claudia.'

'I'm not doubting you,' Susan said consolingly, 'but we must get to the bottom of this. Barry Hearne is looking for information, Marge. Last night when we found him picking at the wax on Icky's paw, I thought he was unduly upset because we caught him.'

'Sue, are you saying that he is at the inn for some other reason besides taking your course?'

'Yes,' Susan replied decisively. 'Just what his game is we can't know until we have more information.'

'I'm beginning to feel very hungry,' said Marge. 'Thinking always affects me that way.'

'And being hit on the head,' Susan chided. 'Do you really feel all right, Marge?'

'Of course I'm all right!' the redhead answered. 'Just hungry. Let's get at that picnic lunch.'

The girls made their way back along the wet, slippery path behind the falls and across to the other side, taking a few moments to again look out through the shimmering, falling water. When they reached the blanket, Susan suddenly stopped and drew in her breath.

'Marge,' she said, her voice tense, 'look! Over there in that field of flowers.'

'Claudia Kingsley and Mrs Tanner, the botanist!' Marge cried.

'Yoohoo!' Mrs Tanner called out, spotting the girls. 'I'm taking some pictures of these lovely daisies, and I insisted that Claudia have her lunch out here with me. We just came from the inn.'

'Sue, how could that be?' Marge Halloran said.

'It's baffling,' responded Susan. 'If Claudia and Mrs Tanner just came from the inn, how could Claudia have been the Phantom? There wouldn't have been time for her to have removed the Indian outfit, gone back to the inn, and returned here.'

'Baffling!' exclaimed Marge. 'It's impossible! I don't see how you can solve this one, Susan Sand!'

6

Black Cloud

'I must solve it, Marge,' said Susan. 'Somehow Claudia played the Phantom, joined Mrs Tanner, and came with her to that field of wild flowers to eat lunch.'

'Sue, it's impossible!' Marge exclaimed. 'She wouldn't have had time.'

'You're certain that the Phantom was Claudia Kingsley?' Susan asked.

'As certain as I can be,' Marge replied. 'But I suppose I could be wrong.'

'No, Marge. I think you knew that Claudia was dressed up in that Indian outfit. We have to discover why she would act in such a peculiar manner and how she could remove the outfit so quickly.'

'Sue, Mrs Tanner just said they were coming *from* the inn,' Marge reminded her. 'So the Phantom couldn't be Claudia, and yet I know she is!'

'Let's invite them over to eat lunch with us,' Susan said quietly. 'We won't say a word about this. Don't reveal to Claudia that you know anything. We must find out the truth!'

Susan Sand called to the pair to come over and join them.

'We'd love to, wouldn't we, Claudia?' Mrs Tanner answered. 'Such a lovely day for a picnic.'

Soon the four were sitting on the blanket, chatting amiably. Claudia was very quiet, her face still pale and her manner restrained. Mrs Tanner, plump and pleasant, talked constantly, and the girls thought they would never have a chance to say anything.

'Edward – that's my hubby – had to go off on business today,' she rambled on. 'He was really mad about it, because we had intended to spend the day with our flowers, but then he got a phone call just after we finished breakfast and so he had to rush right off. He has so many irons in the fire, I sometimes don't even know where he is!'

Mrs Tanner stopped to take a breath.

'I'm glad you managed to get Claudia away from her chores at the inn,' Marge said. 'We wanted her to join us this morning, but she was needed in the dining-room.'

'Well, I just insisted that Claudia come with me. She can't be healthy, staying in that hot kitchen all the time. She has to get out and walk and breathe in this wonderful air and get a change of scene. Aren't I right, Claudia?'

'Yes, Mrs Tanner,' the girl answered. 'It is nice to get out of the kitchen.'

'Oh, I see some big black clouds coming up,' said Mrs Tanner. 'Just when we are in the middle of a nice lunch!'

'Storms come up very quickly in the mountains,' Claudia said in her quiet manner. 'It does look like rain.'

'And the weather was so sunny!' Mrs Tanner continued. 'We are going to be soaked if we don't get back to the inn.'

'Oh, I would say it won't break for twenty minutes or so,' Claudia assured her.

'Well, at least I got some good pictures,' Mrs Tanner said, finishing her sandwich and picking up her camera. 'I think we had better be off, Claudia. I'm sorry to cut this lunch short, girls, but I don't want my precious camera to get wet.'

Mrs Tanner took Claudia's arm, and the pair hurried off towards the inn, the older woman turning about every few steps and waving, until they were out of sight.

'Whew!' exclaimed Marge. 'How she can talk! I don't

39

think it's going to rain all that quickly. She rushed Claudia off as if they had to catch a train.'

'Marge, did you notice traces of make-up in the hair around Claudia's forehead?' Susan asked, her green eyes sparkling.

'Make-up!' Marge cried.

'Yes. Suntan make-up. It was barely discernible, and it was on the side of her head away from us.'

'Well, I didn't see it, Susan Sand,' Marge replied. 'I don't have eyes like a hawk. Then she really was the Phantom!'

'Yes,' Susan said. 'Now we have definite proof that you were right. Claudia Kingsley is the Phantom of the Falls. As for your eyesight, Marge, you were the one who saw through the disguise.'

'I was close to her in the cave behind the falls,' Marge replied. 'You had started to run after Brave Deer.'

'When we solve this mystery, you will deserve a great deal of the credit,' said Susan.

'When "we" solve it!' Marge replied, laughing. 'Sue, I couldn't find the answer to this in three lifetimes.'

'Let's get back to the inn before the deluge,' said Susan, grabbing her friend's hand and pulling her to her feet. 'For someone who was unconscious a short time ago, you seem to be in fine form.'

The two friends gathered up the picnic basket and blanket and started off at a fast pace. The gathering storm clouds rumbled overhead, and the downpour started before the pair had reached the protection of the Feather Inn.

'We're soaked!' cried Marge as the girls climbed the stairs to their rooms. 'We should have listened to Mrs Tanner.'

'The storm was a good excuse for Mrs Tanner to cut short our visit with Claudia,' Susan replied.

'You think she didn't want us to talk to Claudia?'

'Perhaps she was afraid we would notice the make-up.'

'Then she must be in on it, Sue,' Marge reasoned.

'I refuse to jump to conclusions,' the black-haired girl stated. 'But it's something to keep in mind.'

'Oh, there's Icky,' Marge squealed. 'He's drenched. Icky, you look like a drowned rat.'

'Poor Ikhnaton,' said Susan, taking him in her arms. 'How he hates to get wet.'

Once in her room, Susan dried her pet with a large bath-towel and changed her sopping clothes. Soon Icky was reclining on the bed, purring loudly and licking his thick marmalade fur, which had become dishevelled.

'Well, I'm all dried off too,' chuckled Marge, entering her friend's room through the connecting door. 'What a day!'

'There is a great deal of food for thought,' Susan said, lying down next to her cat and placing her hands under her head. 'It seems to me that we have several mysteries to solve. First, why was Barry Hearne up and dressed and prowling about the halls after midnight?'

'And so interested in a piece of wax stuck between Icky's toes?' added Marge.

'Who opened the door on the second floor last night after we found that other bit of wax?' Susan asked.

'And why was Black Cloud, Brave Deer's uncle, running away from the inn at two in the morning, when he should have been with his camping party in the woods?'

'Why is Claudia Kingsley, a shy, timid girl of twelve, dressing up like an Indian boy and scaring Brave Deer out of his wits?' Susan went on.

'And what does Mrs Tanner have to do with it?' Marge added.

'And who hit you over the head, hoping to prevent you from discovering the Phantom was Claudia?' asked Susan, sitting up and looking with her keen eyes at her friend.

'Just a lot of questions, Sue,' Marge cried. 'It's so frustrating! None of it seems to make any sense.'

41

'And we mustn't forget about Barry Hearne,' continued Susan. 'He was trying to find out from us if we knew anything about the Phantom.'

'I wonder how much Mrs Vandervelden knows,' mused Marge.

'She is very fond of Brave Deer,' returned Susan. 'Perhaps he will confide in her.'

At that moment there was a knock on the door.

'Who could that be?' Susan asked, rising from the bed and crossing the room.

When Susan opened the door, both girls were surprised to see a tall, erect, powerfully built Indian of about sixty, dressed in buckskin, standing on the threshold. His face was extremely stern, and in his black eyes was an expression of anger, almost hostility.

'I am Black Cloud,' he began. 'I am sorry to disturb you, Miss Sand, but Mrs Vandervelden said you were at the falls today.'

'Come in, Black Cloud,' said Susan politely, her mind working quickly. 'We haven't met before. This is my friend, Marge Halloran. I thought you were off on a camping trip.'

'We had to return because of the rain,' the Indian replied somewhat impatiently, entering the room. 'It will probably rain for days.'

'Oh, that is too bad,' said Marge.

'One can't quarrel with nature,' Black Cloud said. 'Miss Sand, I must talk to you about my nephew.'

'Black Cloud, I don't know how much Mrs Vandervelden has told you,' Susan began. 'But I don't think it is for me to talk about Brave Deer.'

'Mrs Vandervelden is an old friend of mine,' Black Cloud replied. 'She is a fine woman, and she is trying to help Brave Deer. I know that he ran away from the falls today and that he has been acting strangely for several days. It is very difficult for me to come here and ask your advice, Miss Sand, but you have a reputation as a detective.'

Suddenly the Indian stopped and pointed at the bureau, where Susan had placed the black feather. 'Where did you get that?' he asked sharply, his black eyes narrowing.

'You mean this feather?' Susan replied, picking it up. 'I found it by the falls, near the path on the other side of Feather Creek.'

Black Cloud took the feather from Susan's hand and studied it intently. 'I was wrong to come here,' he said harshly, thrusting the feather back into Susan's hand. 'I am sorry to have disturbed you. I will speak no further about the matter. Good day.'

Black Cloud turned and left the room, closing the door behind him.

'What a formidable man!' Marge whispered.

'He's so impressive,' said Susan Sand. 'How remarkable that he should become frightened at the sight of this feather!'

7

A conversation

'What is different about this feather?' Susan Sand asked.

'It doesn't look different to me,' replied Marge. 'It's just a big black feather.'

'There must be something unusual about it, or Black Cloud would not have acted in such a peculiar manner,' continued Susan.

At that moment there was a knock on the door.

'It's like living in Grand Central Station,' said Marge. 'This time I'll answer it.'

'Mrs Vandervelden!' said Marge in greeting as she opened the door. 'Come in.'

'I hope I'm not disturbing you girls,' said the woman, stepping into the room. 'But I wanted to speak to you.'

'I'm glad you came,' Susan assured her. 'I was about to visit you. How is Brave Deer?'

'He is calmed down,' Mrs Vandervelden replied, sitting in a nearby chair. 'But I am worried, Susan. I have known the boy since he was eight years old, and never have I seen him act in a cowardly manner. When he ran past me out of the cave, he stammered something about a phantom. Yet he refused to say anything more when I questioned him about it. What could be the matter?'

'Has he ever spoken before about this phantom?' Susan asked.

'Not to me,' the woman replied. 'Of course, I arrived only this morning, but Brave Deer was very much himself during my last visit.'

'You seem to be very friendly with his uncle, Black Cloud,' Susan probed.

'Black Cloud is one of the most unusual people I have ever met,' Mrs Vandervelden said. 'He is absolutely fearless, and his knowledge of the woods is astounding. I spoke briefly to him about his nephew's actions at the falls today. He seemed quite disturbed, since Brave Deer has never shown any signs of cowardice.'

'But is it cowardice?' Susan asked.

'Perhaps I am being unfair,' Mrs Vandervelden replied. 'But why should Brave Deer run from the cave in a panic for no reason?'

Susan and Marge glanced at each other.

'I don't believe that Brave Deer is a coward,' Susan stated. 'There is a mystery here that must be solved.'

'Yes, Susan, there is a mystery,' the woman replied, rising. 'It is indeed baffling. I'm sorry to have to leave so suddenly, but Brave Deer and I are going to give Wolf Dog a bath.'

'And I'm going to wash my hair,' replied Marge, laughing, 'and stay out of the rain.'

'Would you girls like to join me for dinner?' Mrs Vandervelden asked. 'I have someone I would like you to meet.'

'Of course,' Susan replied. 'We would love to.'

'Then that's settled,' the woman said, crossing to the door. 'I'll see you tonight about seven.'

'Who does she want us to meet?' asked Marge.

'We'll find out at seven this evening,' Susan replied.

At seven o'clock, Susan and Marge went down to the dining-room. At a table in a corner Mrs Vandervelden was seated with a dark-haired young woman who was a stranger to both the girls. The older woman signalled to them, and they made their way over to the table.

'This is Mrs Karen Minton,' said Mrs Vandervelden. 'Karen, this is the famous Susan Sand and her friend, Marge Halloran.'

'How exciting to meet you and your friend,' Mrs Minton replied, taking Susan's hand. 'I admire your work, Miss Sand.'

'Thank you, Mrs Minton,' Susan replied. 'It's always nice to have someone appreciate your work.'

'You have a reputation as a detective, don't you?' Mrs Minton continued.

'I'll say she does!' Marge exclaimed. 'Did you read in the papers about—'

'Marge,' said Susan, laying a hand on her friend's arm. 'Marge is one of my most fanatical fans.'

'Well, I have a mystery for you,' Mrs Minton continued. 'My apartment on Park Avenue in New York City was robbed today, while my husband and I were off on the camping trip with Black Cloud.'

'Robbed! How awful!' cried Marge. 'Was anything valuable taken?'

'All our art work, our silver, our jewellery, and quite a lot of cash,' Mrs Minton stated. 'My husband rushed off to the city as soon as he received the phone call from our maid. I wanted to go, but he insisted it would just upset me.'

'What is so odd about this is that my apartment was robbed last May, while I was on a camping trip with Black Cloud,' said Mrs Vandervelden.

'And before that, in April, another friend – quite wealthy – was robbed while she and her husband were on a camping trip,' Mrs Minton added in an excited voice. 'They have been coming to the Feather Inn for years.'

'Have the New York City police made any progress?' Susan asked.

'None whatsoever,' Mrs Vandervelden replied. 'They are completely stumped. There were no clues, and whoever entered the apartments didn't even have to break the lock.'

'You mean there was no forced entry?' Marge queried.

'No evidence of one,' Mrs Minton replied.

'Then perhaps it is someone who knows you, someone you wouldn't even suspect,' Susan said.

'I can't imagine any of my friends being thieves!' Mrs Minton exclaimed.

'They certainly wouldn't be a friend,' Mrs Vandervelden replied, laughing. 'I think what Susan meant is that perhaps someone who has access to our apartments has been robbing us.'

'You mean a maid or a delivery man?' Mrs Minton asked.

'Yes,' replied Susan. 'A person who would know when you were going to be away – here at the inn, for instance.'

'That is what my theory has been, Susan,' Mrs Vandervelden said. 'But how does one go about discovering this person?'

'I'm not a policeman,' Susan answered, adjusting her glasses. 'This is a case for the official police department.'

'Yes, Susan, you are right,' sighed Mrs Vandervelden. 'But they have made no progress at all. I thought that, with your experience, you might be able to shed some light on the matter.'

'My only suggestion would be that you should look for one person who knows all of the people who have been robbed,' Susan replied.

'A common denominator.' Mrs Vandervelden mused. 'Yes, Susan, that makes a great deal of sense.'

After dinner the girls excused themselves and returned to Susan's room.

'I like Mrs Vandervelden very much,' said Marge, sitting on the bed and stroking Icky's head. 'But why does she have to pester you with a series of robberies that happened in New York City? I guess that is the price of fame, Susan Sand.'

Susan smiled and sat down on the bed. 'We have enough mystery right here in the Feather Inn,' she replied.

'I'll say we have,' Marge agreed, rising from the bed

and walking over to the window. 'Sue, what could Black Cloud have been doing, running away from the inn last night? Oh, Sue, look! There he is again. Only this time there is someone with him.'

'You mean Black Cloud is running away from the inn again?' Susan asked, hurrying to the window.

'No, he's not running. He's talking with someone over in the shadows by those trees. Who is the other man?'

'It's Barry Hearne!' Susan cried as the figure turned his head. 'Black Cloud and Barry Hearne standing out there in the pouring rain!'

'They seem to be whispering about something,' said Marge. 'Why are they hiding among those trees as if they don't want to be seen?'

8

An Odega chronicle

'They act very secretive,' said Susan Sand, looking out the window at Black Cloud and Barry Hearne. 'What could those two men have in common that could cause them to meet in the pouring rain and whisper like conspirators?'

'Perhaps they are conspirators,' answered Marge. 'Maybe Barry Hearne did hit me over the head to prevent me from discovering the identity of the Phantom.'

'And Black Cloud is in on it?' Susan asked. 'It seems most unlikely, Marge, that Black Cloud would be involved in such a scheme. Yet we really know very little about him, except that he is a noted woodsman and a very impressive person.'

'I am going to wash my hair and try to forget about it,' Marge announced. 'Maybe tomorrow it will all come clear.'

'If only the rain would stop, we could return to the falls and investigate the spot where we saw Claudia as the Phantom,' lamented Susan.

But the following morning the rain was still falling heavily, and the two friends decided that outdoor detective work would have to be postponed.

'Let's go into the town of Featherford,' Susan suggested. 'There is a Crafts Centre and a little museum run by the Odega Indians. An Indian woman by the name of Rose Petal is curator of the museum. She has great knowledge of Odega history and might be able to help us.'

Susan and Marge donned raincoats, hats, and boots and set out for Featherford in Susan's car.

'Sue,' said Marge, her voice low, 'there is a car following us, and the driver is Barry Hearne.'

'Barry Hearne!' exclaimed Susan. 'Are you certain he is following us?'

'He is giving a very good imitation of it,' replied Marge, craning her neck. 'I spotted him right after we left the inn, but I didn't say anything until we made that last turn. He's been right behind us all the way.'

'How very interesting!' replied Susan Sand, smiling mischievously.

'He likes you, Sue,' Marge teased. 'Only he's the bashful kind who can't bring himself to approach you openly.'

'So that's what you think, Marge Halloran?' retorted Susan, turning her head briefly and shooting a keen glance at her friend. 'I'm more inclined to believe that his motives are other than romantic.'

'Always the sleuth!' Marge chided, her face assuming an innocent expression. 'Wait until Professor Scott hears that you have another admirer.'

When the girls arrived in the town of Featherford and parked on the main street, Barry Hearne pulled up behind them.

'He is making no effort to conceal his interest now,' Susan noted. 'I think he is planning to join us.'

'Hello, Miss Sand, Miss Halloran,' the man said cheerfully, striding towards them. 'Lovely day for fish!'

'Does he think he is being funny?' Marge said. 'He's all yours, Sue. I'm going to stay completely out of this.'

'Good day, Mr Hearne,' said Susan pleasantly. 'I see you had the same idea as we did on how to spend a rainy day.'

'Are you going to visit the Crafts Centre?' the man asked in his genial manner.

'Of course,' Susan answered. 'And you?'

'Our minds run in the same direction,' he replied. 'I

intend to buy an Indian blanket. I'm sure you won't mind if I join you.'

'Not at all,' responded Susan, adjusting her glasses as the trio started towards a row of shops which displayed various Indian objects in their windows.

For at least an hour they went in and out of the many shops, scrutinising the numerous pieces of jewellery, beaded belts, moccasins, hand-carved figures, clay pottery and pipes, beautiful jackets, and blankets. At one point Barry Hearne selected a lovely blanket in a variety of earth tones.

'I like your choice, Mr Hearne,' said Susan. 'If you hadn't bought that particular blanket, I would have.'

'Then you must let me make you a present of it,' he insisted, offering her the package.

'Mr Hearne, you know I won't accept a present from a man I hardly know,' Susan replied firmly.

Marge could not help giggling, and Susan nudged her with an elbow.

'Very well,' Barry Hearne said. 'Then I will just have to keep this blanket until I get to know you better.'

'We are going on to the museum, Mr Hearne,' Susan answered coolly.

She managed to pull Marge some distance ahead of their attentive escort. 'Did you see the Tanners back there in that jewellery shop?' she asked in a subdued voice.

'No. You mean they are following us too?' Marge replied.

'I don't know if they are tailing us, but Mr Tanner nodded to me,' Susan said.

'Am I missing out on a secret?' Barry Hearne asked, catching up with them.

'Nothing important,' Susan retorted. 'Here we are at the museum.'

The only person in the small room was a tall, broad-faced Indian woman with braided black hair, and an intricately woven shawl around her shoulders.

'How nice to see you again, Miss Sand,' she said cordially.

'Hello, Rose Petal,' Susan greeted her. 'This is my friend, Marge Halloran, and this is Mr Hearne, who is also staying at the inn.'

'Good day to you,' Rose Petal replied. 'Please take your time and look over our exhibits. We do not have a great deal on display, but I think you will find it interesting. If you have any questions, don't hesitate to ask.'

'Thank you,' Susan answered. 'I would like to know something about Odega history. I am always seeking information for my books.'

'What would you particularly like to know about the Odegas?' Rose Petal asked. 'Our history goes back over three hundred and fifty years.'

'Were your people always in this area?' Susan asked.

'Oh, yes. Originally the Odegas were part of another tribe, but a rift took place over hunting rights, and we broke off and formed our own tribe. There was a great deal of warring between tribes in the sixteen-thirties. So much, in fact, that a Council of Seven Chiefs was created to try to bring peace. The chief of the Odegas was named Wahenatha. He was a very great man and knew that Indians must be at peace among themselves if they were to deal with the white man.'

'I have heard of Chief Wahenatha,' said Susan. 'His idea was really a United Nations, wasn't it?'

'An early version of it,' Rose Petal answered, laughing. 'The other six tribes realised how wise his idea was, and they agreed to have a meeting in the cavern behind the Featherford Falls in order to form the council. Unfortunately, there was one tribe, the Dayonas, which was against any kind of peace. They had always been extremely warlike and wanted no part of the council.

'Chief Wahenatha knew that his main problem would be the Dayonas, which is the reason that the meeting of the Council of Seven Chiefs was to take place in the cavern behind the falls. The meeting could be held secretly, and a calumet or Pipe of Peace was fashioned by an Odega craftsman. The bowl of the pipe was made of clay and fired by him. It was elaborately painted and decorated, and the reed stem, which was over two feet long, was enhanced with many feathers. The calumet was truly a work of art, and it has been talked about down through the centuries.'

'What happened to the Pipe of Peace?' Marge asked. 'I should think it would be very valuable.'

'The story of the Pipe of Peace is the sad part of our history,' Rose Petal continued. 'No one has ever known what happened to it. A young brave by the name of White Rabbit, who was the brother of an ancestor of Black Cloud and Brave Deer, was to bring the pipe at night to the cavern behind the falls, so that it would not fall into the hands of the Dayonas. White Rabbit was a noted runner and only about fourteen.

'The pipe was placed in a cedar box and then wrapped carefully in a deerskin sack, which White Rabbit carried on his back so that he could run without any hindrance. He started out for the cavern from an undisclosed location, but he never reached the Council of Seven Chiefs waiting for him behind the falling water.'

'What happened to him?' Barry Hearne blurted out.

'No one knows, Mr Hearne,' Rose Petal answered, her face solemn. 'All sorts of stories have come down to us. Unfortunately, the most famous one is that White Rabbit was a coward and that he was attacked by the Dayonas. It has been said that he gave them the Pipe of Peace in exchange for his own life.'

'Was he never questioned about it?' Susan asked.

'He was never seen again, Miss Sand,' the Indian woman explained. 'What happened that night has remained a mystery all through the years. White Rabbit set out on his mission with the Pipe of Peace tied securely

53

to his back, but he never reached the cavern, and neither he nor the pipe was ever seen again.'

'How extraordinary!' Marge exclaimed.

'What happened to the Council of Seven Chiefs and the plans for peace?' Susan asked.

'Oh, peace came about, despite the Dayonas and their warlike ways,' Rose Petal said. 'The Pipe of Peace was meant to be a symbol and was to be smoked by the seven chiefs in a gesture of friendship. Even without the calumet, an agreement was reached, and the council brought peace to the entire area. But White Rabbit's name has never been cleared.'

'Were there any clues at the time to explain what could have occurred?' Susan asked.

'None that have come down to us. There was an incident that night that some people thought might have been connected with White Rabbit's disappearance. There was a white man by the name of William Smythe. He was a farmer who owned a stone farmhouse not far from the Feather Inn. In fact, the building is still standing. The day after White Rabbit and the Pipe of Peace disappeared, Farmer Smythe was found dead, lying on the floor of his farmhouse. He had been killed by the Dayonas. One of their arrows was found in his body, but no one has ever been able to explain why he was killed.'

'Then there are people who think that there could have been a connection between his death and White Rabbit's disappearance,' Susan deduced.

'Yes, Miss Sand,' Rose Petal agreed. 'Farmer Smythe was a friend of the Odegas and the other six tribes of this area. But he was a special friend to the Odegas, so some people assumed that he was connected with White Rabbit's disappearance. No proof was ever found, however.'

Everyone remained silent for several moments after Rose Petal had finished her story. Suddenly she got up from the stool where she had been seated and went to a cabinet in one corner of the room.

'There was an item on display for many years which related to this story,' she said, opening the cabinet. 'But we removed it because some Odegas objected. It's a big black feather that belonged to a bird no longer found in this area. To the Odegas, this black feather is a symbol of cowardice. This particular feather is very old, although not as old as the story I have just told you. It was on display, along with a description of the story of White Rabbit and the Pipe of Peace. Perhaps you would like to see it?'

'Indeed we would,' said Susan, her green eyes sparkling.

'It's not here!' Rose Petal cried, reaching far back into the cabinet. 'I had placed it very carefully in a box. Miss Sand, the feather is missing!'

9

Forgotten evidence

'The box is not here,' cried Rose Petal, searching every corner of the cabinet. 'Someone has taken it. Who would want to steal a black feather?'

'Do you usually leave the cabinet open?' asked Susan Sand, peering into the recess.

'Yes,' Rose Petal answered. 'I never thought of locking it. I see now it was very careless of me.'

At that moment the door of the museum opened, and Mr and Mrs Tanner entered.

'Hello!' Mrs Tanner exclaimed, waving to the group. 'How nice to meet you here! My goodness, it's still raining, so we thought we'd make another visit to this interesting museum.'

'Something wrong?' Mr Tanner asked. 'You all look kind of upset.'

'Someone has stolen the black feather that I showed to you last week,' Rose Petal explained.

'Stolen the black feather?' Mr Tanner replied, his eyebrows rising. 'Who would want to do that?'

'How terrible!' Mrs Tanner chimed in. 'That feather means a lot to the Odegas, as you told us, Rose Petal.'

'I wouldn't worry too much about it, Rose Petal,' said Mr Tanner consolingly. 'After all, you told us that the feather was only a symbol.'

'Yes, that's true,' the Indian agreed. 'But it is disturbing to think of someone coming in here and actually stealing it.'

'Is there anyone else who works here who might have taken it?' Barry Hearne asked.

'There are two other people who help out in the museum,' replied Rose Petal. 'But if they wanted the feather for some reason, which seems most unlikely, they would certainly ask me.'

'When was the last time you looked in this cabinet?' Susan asked.

'Last week, when I showed the feather to the Tanners,' replied Rose Petal. 'We don't have a great many people come here, and when they do, they often don't want to listen to me. They just stroll through and make comments about the exhibits and then leave.'

'Please don't be upset,' said Susan to the Indian woman. 'I promise that I will do all I can to clear this matter up.'

'If only you could, Miss Sand,' Rose Petal said. 'Even though the feather has no monetary value, it does have a great deal of historical significance. I would like to get it back. It would be next to impossible to find another one, since the species of bird that dropped it is no longer in this area.'

Susan glanced at Marge, whose face betrayed her inner feelings of guilt at possessing a feather that was most likely the one in question. The redhead, however, kept her silence. Her past experience with Susan Sand had taught her that such an important clue must be concealed until the mystery was solved.

'We have to get back to the inn, Rose Petal,' said Susan, starting for the door. 'But I promise that I will not forget about this.'

'Thank you, Miss Sand. And thank you, Miss Halloran and Mr Hearne, for being so interested in our history.'

'My pleasure,' Barry Hearne replied. 'You have a very informative little museum here, and I think that more people should take advantage of it.'

Rose Petal smiled and escorted the trio to the door after they bade farewell to the Tanners.

'What do you make of that?' asked Barry Hearne. 'Stealing a black feather! What for?'

'It is peculiar,' Susan answered. 'Have you no theories, Mr Hearne?'

'Perhaps someone's aunt wants to make a hat,' he replied, chuckling.

'I don't think it's funny,' replied Marge, her face flushing. 'That feather means a lot to the Odegas. I wouldn't laugh about it.'

'I was only kidding,' the big man replied. 'But I can't understand what all the fuss is about.'

'You just told Rose Petal how interesting the museum is,' Susan reminded him.

'I meant it. It *is* interesting, but I don't think the loss of one old black feather could be that important.'

'You and I think very differently, Mr Hearne,' said Susan, taking Marge's arm and starting for her car.

'I'll see you back at the inn,' he replied, shrugging his shoulders. 'I have a feeling you are trying to get rid of me.'

Barry Hearne chuckled again and strode towards his car, the package containing the Indian blanket firmly under his arm.

'Ooh, he's so forward,' said Marge. 'Imagine wanting to give you that blanket! He hardly knows you.'

'Don't be taken in by Mr Hearne, Marge,' Susan warned.

'Do you think *he* might have stolen the feather?'

'Certainly he might have. So might the Tanners, or a dozen other people. Since Rose Petal never locked the cabinet, anyone could have stolen it.'

'But if the missing feather is the same one that you found by the falls, then Claudia must have taken it,' Marge stated.

'Claudia, or someone else forcing her to play the Phantom,' Susan replied.

58

'Then you think there is someone behind Claudia?' Marge asked.

'We must consider that possibility,' Susan said as the girls climbed into the car. 'Claudia is very timid and frightened. I don't think she would play such a role on her own.'

'What do you plan to do now, Sue?' Marge asked.

'Go back to the Feather Inn and call Randall Scott.'

'How can Professor Scott help us?'

'Since he is an American history scholar, he might know quite a bit about the Odegas,' Susan replied, starting the engine and pulling out of the parking place. 'By the way, I put the black feather in an envelope in my purse. I intend to carry it around with me so no one else can take it.'

As soon as Susan reached the inn, she called Randall Scott from the telephone in the lobby.

'How good to hear your voice,' he said. 'Did the seminar go well?'

'Very well, Randall,' Susan replied. 'But I called you about something else. Do you know anything about the Odega Indians?'

'The Odegas? Yes, quite a bit. What do they have to do with your seminar?'

'Nothing,' Susan answered, laughing. 'Something has come up, and I need your advice.'

'By "something coming up" you mean you have found another mystery,' Randall Scott said astutely.

'Yes, I have. An extremely intriguing one.'

'Now listen, Susan Sand. I have got into a great deal of trouble through you and your mysteries. But since you have managed to solve them all, and since I am still alive, I will consent to see you about this one. Come to my office at Irongate today, if you can. I'll have a surprise for you.'

'A surprise? What do you mean?'

'I'll tell you when you get here.'

'Marge and I will leave right away. We'll be there in several hours.'

By four o'clock that afternoon, Susan and Marge were seated in Randall Scott's office in Piper Hall, the building that housed the History Department of Irongate University. Brian Lorenzo, a young research assistant of Professor Scott's and a special friend of Marge's, was also present.

Randall Scott, a handsome young man with rugged features and wavy brown hair, was the Chairman of the History Department, the youngest person ever to be appointed to that post. His fame was not confined to Irongate, however, since he was the author of several books on American history and had given many lectures throughout the country and in Europe as well.

Brian Lorenzo, one of his students and his main research assistant, was tall and lean with curly black hair and black eyes that betrayed his good humour. His delight at seeing Marge was badly concealed, and the redhead's freckles seemed all the more prominent as she blushed under his scrutiny.

'So now you are entangled with the Odega Indians,' said Randall Scott, his brown eyes smiling mischievously at Susan. 'I thought you went to Featherford Falls to teach a course on the art of the detective story.'

'I did, Randall, but we have come across the most fascinating mystery,' Susan began exuberantly. 'I brought this black feather with me. It seems to be at the centre of the whole thing.'

Susan opened her purse and placed the feather on the young man's desk. Clearly and concisely she related everything that had happened. Both men listened eagerly until she had finished her recital.

'Do you mean to tell me that Barry Hearne has been following you around in his car?' asked Randall Scott. 'Who is he, and what is his interest in this?'

The young man could not conceal his anger, and Marge was forced to turn her head in order to hide her amusement.

'He followed us from the Feather Inn,' Susan replied. 'He's outside now, or he was when we came in. I don't know who he is, Randall.'

Professor Scott rose from his chair and strode quickly to the window. He was tall and broad-shouldered and carried himself like an athlete.

'He's hanging around by his car,' he said, pulling aside the curtain. 'What nerve! I'd like to say a few words to him right now.'

'Please, Randall, don't get upset,' Susan pleaded. 'In a way, it's my fault, since I encouraged him in order to get information.'

'Suppose he's dangerous?' Randall Scott asked. 'Maybe he's the one who hit Marge over the head.'

'He was on the spot,' Susan agreed. 'But so was Mrs Tanner. Randall, it could have been almost anyone. The area around the falls is all woods. Hiding would be easy. What is the surprise you mentioned on the phone?'

'Oh, yes,' said Professor Scott, crossing over to his desk and opening a drawer. 'It's a diary. William Smythe's diary, as a matter of fact.'

He took out a small leatherbound volume and handed it to Susan.

'William Smythe!' exclaimed Susan, taking the diary and thumbing through it. 'He was the farmer who was found dead in his farmhouse after White Rabbit disappeared. How is it that you have his diary?'

'It was left to Irongate University many years ago,' Brian explained. 'It's been all but forgotten, locked away in Van Delft Library. After you phoned, Professor Scott went and got it from the archives.'

'How exciting, Sue!' cried Marge, getting up and coming over to Susan's chair. 'Maybe it will give us a clue.'

'I read through it before you arrived,' said Professor Scott. 'There is one very interesting part. You said that White Rabbit was considered a coward, since people thought he gave the Pipe of Peace to the Dayonas in exchange for his own life. Just read this excerpt from Farmer Smythe.'

Randall Scott had crossed over to Susan's chair and opened the diary to a certain page. Susan scanned it quickly and read aloud:

'And inasmuch as I have come to know White Rabbit very well, I consider him to be a brave and intelligent young Odega of which the tribe may well be proud. He has proven himself in many ways and possesses traits of leadership.'

'So you see, according to Farmer Smythe, White Rabbit was anything but a coward,' commented Professor Scott.

'I wonder if the Odega Indians know about this,' said Susan.

'Probably not,' Randall Scott replied. 'The diary really should be in the museum in Featherford.'

'White Rabbit has come down through history as a coward when he wasn't,' Marge stated. 'What could have happened that night of the meeting of the Council of Seven Chiefs?'

'A mystery over three hundred years old!' said Brian. 'Quite a challenge, Sue!'

'But it must be solved,' said Susan Sand, adjusting her glasses and re-reading Farmer Smythe's writing. 'The black feather is a symbol of cowardice to the Odegas. For some reason, Claudia Kingsley has been dressing up as a young Indian and wearing this black feather in her headband in order to frighten Brave Deer.'

'How does that relate to a peace pipe and a young Indian who disappeared over three centuries ago?' asked Brian.

'White Rabbit was the younger brother of an ancestor of Black Cloud and Brave Deer,' Susan replied. 'I think I see a pattern evolving.'

Susan Sand looked at the black feather lying on Randall Scott's desk. 'Claudia Kingsley is very fond of Brave Deer, and yet she has been the means of frightening him away from the falls,' she continued.

'You think there is someone behind her, making her do it,' said Professor Scott.

'Yes,' Susan replied heatedly. 'And that person or persons know about the black feather and White Rabbit and the entire history of the Odegas and are making use of it. It's a cruel plot, and we must discover who is responsible, and why!'

10

A fraud unmasked

'We have conflicting evidence,' said Susan Sand, studying Farmer Smythe's diary. 'According to Odega history, White Rabbit was a coward. According to Farmer Smythe, he was a brave Indian who had leadership qualities. Which is the truth?'

'The only way to find the truth is to discover what happened the night of the meeting of the Council of Seven Chiefs,' replied Professor Scott. 'The Pipe of Peace of the Odega Indians has been lost for over three centuries. There have been efforts to find it, but without success. Unless the truth of that night is known, White Rabbit's name will always be tarnished.'

'Yes, Randall,' agreed Susan, adjusting her glasses. 'Finding the Pipe of Peace would be a great step, but still it wouldn't clear White Rabbit's name. We still wouldn't know what happened.'

'Perhaps he was killed by the Dayonas,' offered Brian. 'They were an extremely warlike tribe.'

'That seems the most likely explanation,' replied Susan. 'The fact that Farmer Smythe was found dead in his farmhouse the very next day seems to indicate that he might have known something. But how can one find clues after all this time?'

'It seems an impossible task,' said Randall Scott. 'But the subject is so interesting, I would like to join in the investigation. How would it suit you if I came to the Feather Inn?'

'Wonderful, Randall!' Susan exclaimed.

'Hey, don't leave me out!' cried Brian.

'Of course not, silly,' said Marge. 'We can all look for the peace pipe together.'

'I hope you can get a room,' said Susan. 'According to Mr Kingsley, the inn is full. You'd better call him, Randall.'

Randall Scott crossed to his desk and picked up the telephone. Susan gave him the number, and soon he was talking to Warren Kingsley.

'We're in luck,' he said, placing the phone on the receiver. 'The inn is full, but there is a small house that Mr Kingsley has just bought and is renovating. He said that if we don't mind some inconvenience, he could put us up there. Apparently only one room is finished.'

'Suits me fine,' said Brian. 'Camping out in the woods would be even more fun.'

'Brian, that's not a bad idea,' chimed in Marge. 'Perhaps we could all go on a camping trip with Black Cloud. The rain is bound to stop sometime.'

'Great!' answered Brian. 'I'll bring my sleeping-bag.'

'I've heard of Black Cloud,' said Professor Scott. 'He knows more about the woods than anybody in this entire area. Camping out would be fun.'

'Oh, good!' cried Marge. 'Why don't you all come to Hollowhearth House for dinner, and we can leave for the inn in the morning.'

'We can buy pizzas,' suggested Brian. 'I'm sure your mother wouldn't like us barging in on her at dinnertime.'

'Perfect!' agreed Marge. 'I'll call home right now.'

Marge talked to her mother on the phone, and plans were made for the group to go to Hollowhearth House.

'Mother wants your Aunt Adele to come if she can,' said Marge to Susan.

'I intend to go home now anyway, so I'll see if she is busy or if she can spare some time,' said Susan.

'And I want to stop by the bookshop,' stated Marge.

'We have Mr Jenkins running it now, but I still feel responsible.'

'Let me take you in my car,' said Brian. 'Then Susan can go home and bring her aunt to Hollowhearth House for dinner.'

'Everything is settled,' said Susan Sand. 'Perhaps we'll be able to get to the bottom of this and discover who is frightening Brave Deer and why.'

'And find the Pipe of Peace and what happened to White Rabbit and why Farmer Smythe was killed,' added Brian, smiling broadly. 'And why Claudia Kingsley is masquerading as an Indian.'

'You don't think Susan can do it, do you, Brian?' Marge asked in a challenging voice. 'Well, I think she can, especially with the help of two famous historians.'

The two men laughed good-naturedly as Randall Scott strode over to the window.

'I'd like to know what that Barry Hearne has to do with this,' he said. 'His car is gone. I wonder where he went?'

'He tried to give Susan a beautiful Indian blanket he bought at the Crafts Centre,' said Marge, glancing at Susan.

'What!' Randall Scott cried, turning around. 'An Indian blanket! Why, Susan, he hardly knows you. I hope you didn't accept it.'

'Of course not, Randall,' replied Susan, rising from her chair. 'I don't think that Mr Hearne's interest in me is restricted to offering me gifts.'

'Then what is his interest in you?'

'I'm not quite sure,' she replied, narrowing her eyes. 'But he seems to be looking for information, just the way we are.'

'Well, I don't trust him,' Professor Scott said angrily. 'I'm glad to be going to the inn. With someone like that hanging around, there's no telling what might happen.'

Several hours later the entire group was settled comfortably at Hollowhearth House, enjoying pizzas and listening to Winifred Halloran, Marge's mother, expound on the delights of living in a historic building. She was a small, pretty woman with grey hair and intelligent blue eyes.

'If it weren't for Susan, we wouldn't be living here at all,' she said, sipping her coffee. 'We can never thank you enough, Sue.'

'She solved her first case, and we got Hollowhearth House,' said Marge, taking another chunk of pizza. 'Just last month there was an article in *The Thornewood Times* about how mother and I live in this part of the house and show the rest as a museum by having tours three times a week. What a lot of valuable stuff there is!'

'There are two wonderful paintings by Colonial artists,' said Adele Sand, Susan's aunt, who was a professor of art history at Irongate University. She was a tall, handsome woman with grey hair, and Susan bore a striking resemblance to her.

'Between the Thornewood Bookshop and Hollow-hearth House, you must be kept very busy, Mrs Halloran,' said Susan.

'Indeed we are, Susan,' Mrs Halloran replied. 'But since we employed that pleasant and efficient fellow Kenneth Jenkins, I've had more time to devote to the house.'

'I stopped by the shop this afternoon, Mother,' said Marge, her words somewhat distorted because her mouth was full of pizza. 'Mr Jenkins seems very happy in his job. You know, Sue, someone came in and bought that book by the Tanners on wild flowers.'

'Really!' exclaimed Susan, leaning forward in her chair. 'What a coincidence! Just yesterday morning we were talking to the Tanners about their books.'

'Talking to the Tanners!' exclaimed Mrs Halloran. 'But, Susan, the Tanners are dead!'

'Dead!' the group cried together.

'Yes, dead. I remember the book you mentioned,

Marge,' Mrs Halloran explained. 'There was a biographical sketch on the back which stated that the Tanners were English botanists who lived in America for several years while they were writing a book on the wild flowers of North America. They died in England well into their eighties.'

'Then who are the two people at the Feather Inn?' Marge asked.

'Mrs Halloran, are you quite certain of your facts?' asked Susan.

'Positive, Sue,' Mrs Halloran stated. 'I am very interested in flowers, and I remember that book well.'

'Then those two people at the Feather Inn who are calling themselves Eunice and Edward Tanner must be frauds!' Susan exclaimed. 'I wonder what the person who bought the book on wild flowers looked like.'

'Mr Jenkins mentioned his appearance because he thought the man looked odd,' answered Marge. 'He was wearing a raincoat and a hat, even though it was so hot yesterday morning. He said he had a black beard.'

'He sounds like someone out of a spy movie,' offered Brian.

'It certainly was too hot to be wearing a raincoat and a hat,' observed Susan.

'Do you think that he could have been the bogus Mr Tanner wearing a false beard?' Adele Sand asked.

'That is very possible,' answered Susan. 'Yesterday morning Marge and I met the "Tanners" on the way to breakfast. Marge mentioned that she knew she had one of their books in her bookshop. Since Mr Tanner appears to be masquerading as a person who is dead, he must have become frightened that his deception would be uncovered. He thought someone might read the biographical sketch on the real Tanners on the back of the book, so he rushed off to Thornewood in disguise to buy it.'

'Whatever his game is, it's a very dangerous one,' said Randall Scott.

'When we return to the inn, we must not let on in any way that we have unmasked them,' Susan Sand stated in a determined voice. 'We must discover what they are doing at the inn, and why they have taken the names of two respectable English people who are now dead.'

'What a lot of gall they have!' said Brian. 'They were bound to be found out.'

'Mrs Tanner was with Claudia Kingsley yesterday, not long after we saw the Phantom,' Susan stated.

'I'd say the "Tanners" are high on the list of suspects,' said Randall Scott.

'But what are they doing at the inn, masquerading as the Tanners?' repeated Susan, rising from her chair. 'If they are responsible for Claudia playing the Phantom, there must be a reason for it. I never tried to solve a mystery with so many angles.'

'You will solve it, Sue,' Professor Scott assured her. 'And I'll be there to help you.'

11

A clue in the dust

The following morning Susan Sand rose early. She and her Aunt Adele lived in a charming old stone house just off the campus of Irongate University, where Adele Sand was a professor. Susan descended the stairs and entered the dining-room to find her aunt talking animatedly to Mrs Draper, the Sands' housekeeper and cook.

'Good morning, Sue,' Adele Sand greeted her. 'Mrs Draper and I were just discussing your latest case.'

'Imagine, Susan, those fake Tanners parading around pretending to be botanists!' exclaimed Mrs Draper, placing Susan's breakfast before her. 'Whatever could they be up to?'

'I intend to find out,' replied Susan, hurriedly eating her bacon and eggs. 'I'm going to visit Chief Burton at police headquarters before we leave for Featherford Falls. He might be able to help me discover who they really are. Please say nothing about this to anyone, Mrs Draper.'

'Oh, Susan, you can trust me,' the housekeeper answered. 'I know how important your cases are. I won't breathe a word to anyone.'

'Susan, why should the "Tanners" take the name of two respected people?' Professor Sand asked, looking with her keen grey eyes at her niece. 'Certainly they risk being found out, which is exactly what has occurred. Why not just assume an alias?'

'I suspect they needed a convincing front, Aunt Adele,' Susan explained. 'If they have done this before and have

70

a criminal record, Chief Burton will be able to trace them.'

Susan quickly finished her breakfast and drove to police headquarters. Douglas Burton, Chief of the Thornewood Police Department, rose to greet her as she entered his office. He was a big, burly man with a brusque manner, but his rather forbidding countenance softened when he saw Susan.

'Susan Sand, I haven't seen you in a long time,' he said cordially, taking her hand. 'The last time we worked together was on the Clovercrest Castle case. How have you been?'

'Fine, Chief,' Susan replied, smiling warmly at him. 'I have come to ask a favour. Perhaps you won't be able to help me, since my latest case isn't in your jurisdiction.'

Briefly Susan related the duplicity of the false Tanners and her adventure at Featherford Falls. Chief Burton listened attentively and made a few notes on a pad on his desk. He asked for a physical description of the Tanners and carefully jotted it down.

'They're phonies, all right,' he said, tapping his pencil on the blotter. 'They sound like real pros. I'll look into this, Susan. When you are in law enforcement, certain people keep popping up. I'd say that the bogus Tanners might have a record. If they do, I'll be able to identify them for you.'

'I would be extremely grateful,' Susan replied.

'I couldn't turn you down, Susan,' he answered. 'You've been valuable to me in the past, and I don't want to lose a good detective. If I find out anything, I'll contact you at the falls.'

Susan thanked Chief Burton and returned to her car. As she started the engine she saw a maroon sedan pull away from the kerb and turn the corner some distance down the street from police headquarters.

'Barry Hearne!' said Susan, adjusting her glasses and peering through the windshield. 'He's being more cagey. I don't believe he wanted to be seen. Why is he following me around?'

Within an hour, Susan had picked up Marge at Hollowhearth House and, followed by Brian Lorenzo and Randall Scott in the professor's car, the friends started for Featherford Falls.

'So Barry Hearne followed you to the police station,' said Marge.

'Yes, but surreptitiously this time.'

'Did you tell Professor Scott?'

'No, I didn't,' Susan retorted. 'I don't want him jumping to conclusions about Barry Hearne. He might do something rash. Please keep the information to yourself, Marge.'

'Randall is very protective towards you, Sue,' replied the redhead. 'I should think Barry Hearne might become jealous.'

'I do not look upon Mr Hearne as a possible suitor,' Susan rejoined, wrinkling her nose. 'Tailing me to a police station is hardly a romantic act.'

The sun was shining brightly when the two cars reached the Feather Inn, and the day promised to be very hot. Icky rushed from some bushes to greet his mistress and leapt in the air several times to show his delight.

'Ikhnaton!' cried Randall Scott, picking him up and holding him above his head. 'Have you been investigating the woods? Your feet are muddy, and your fur is all matted.'

'He needs a good combing,' replied Susan. 'The country is not the best place for Icky.'

Mr Kingsley greeted his two new guests and insisted on taking them personally to their temporary quarters.

'I am sorry there is no room here at the inn,' he apologised. 'Smythe House is not far. I am having it renovated, but there is one room ready that I am certain you will find quite comfortable.'

72

'By Smythe House do you mean the old farmhouse that was once owned by William Smythe?' Susan asked.

'Yes, Susan, the very house,' Warren Kingsley replied.

'Then the house is very old,' said Brian.

'Oh, very,' Mr Kingsley agreed. 'And very historical. I plan to restore it and make it a showplace, but there is a great deal of work still to be done.'

'What do you mean by historical?' Susan asked, glancing at her friends as they walked down a narrow country lane towards a stone house that stood among trees several hundred feet away.

'Farmer Smythe was a friend of the Odega Indians,' replied the hotel owner. 'He was killed by a warring tribe in this very house. I plan to have a little booklet printed for distribution to our guests with a complete history of the house.'

'We are grateful to have a place to stay,' Randall Scott said, winking at Susan.

The Smythe farmhouse was a Colonial structure of two storeys, with small, recessed windows set in stone. Two narrow brick steps led up to the front door, which stood open, revealing several workmen inside.

'They are repairing the floor,' said Mr Kingsley. 'I think it better if we enter by the rear door, since there are stairs which go directly up to the room where you will stay.'

The group followed their host around the side of the house and into the back entrance.

'I will give you the key to this door,' he said, leading the way up a winding staircase and into a room at the top. 'I hope you will be comfortable. Several people have already stayed here. Mr Hearne slept here for three nights just two weeks ago, and the Tanners stayed one night only last week.'

'It looks very pleasant,' commented Randall Scott, placing his suitcase on the floor.

'There is a new bathroom which I had put in,' said

Mr Kingsley, crossing the room and opening a door.

'Very nice,' said Brian, flinging himself on one of the beds.

'And the mattresses are new,' added the manager proudly. 'I've been told they are extremely comfortable.'

'This is a very interesting house,' said Susan Sand, looking out one of the windows. 'Didn't these windows once have inside shutters?'

'You are absolutely right, Susan,' said Mr Kingsley. 'Many of the houses built back in early Colonial days did have wooden shutters on the inside. Much warmer, you see.'

'And much safer in case of Indian attacks,' said Professor Scott. 'They could be closed across the windows and fastened.'

'You said that Barry Hearne and the Tanners stayed in this room?' Susan queried.

'Yes, Susan, but I moved them into the inn just as soon as we had a vacancy,' Mr Kingsley explained. 'Mrs Tanner's only complaint was that there wasn't enough closet space. There is only one small closet, but I plan to make the storage room into another as soon as I have the old shutters moved out.'

Mr Kingsley crossed over to another door and opened it, disclosing a long, dusty space under slanting eaves.

'Why, it's full of window shutters,' said Susan. 'Are they the original shutters, Mr Kingsley?'

'Yes, I think so,' he replied. 'And they are all in good condition. For some reason a former owner took them down and stored them in here. I intend to have them painted and replaced, but not until the more important work is done. I don't believe anyone has been in this storage room for many, many years.'

'But the dust is all disturbed,' Marge blurted out.

'Why, so it is, Miss Halloran,' replied Mr Kingsley. 'My workmen must have been in here after all.'

Susan Sand stepped into the storage room and looked

74

about. Large cobwebs hung from the ceiling, and the single window was covered with grime.

'Susan, I am not sure that the floor is quite safe in there,' said Mr Kingsley, motioning for her to come out. 'I really think I should keep this door locked until the room has been renovated.'

'Of course,' replied Susan, stepping back into the bedroom.

Mr Kingsley locked the door and put the key in his pocket. Then he wished them good day and left to return to the Feather Inn.

'Sue, what is it?' asked Randall Scott, noting the puzzled expression on her face.

'There is a used flashbulb lying in a crack between two of the floorboards,' Susan replied, brushing a strand of raven hair from her forehead. 'It looked too clean to have been there long.'

'A used flashbulb!' Brian exclaimed. 'Who would be taking pictures in a room full of old window shutters?'

'And now the door is locked, and I can't get in to investigate!' lamented Susan Sand.

12

The secret of the Phantom

'Why did Mr Kingsley suddenly lock the door?' asked Marge.

'Perhaps he saw the flashbulb, too,' offered Brian.

'The reason he gave could be genuine,' said Susan Sand. 'The floor may really be unsafe. But that flashbulb didn't just fly in through the window. Someone was taking pictures in that storage room, and not long ago.'

'Maybe we could pick the lock,' suggested Brian.

'What a silly suggestion,' chided Marge. 'Then Mr Kingsley might notice that we had tampered with it.'

'And what, may I ask, do you propose, Miss Halloran?' Brian rejoined.

'I propose a trip to the Featherford Falls,' interrupted Susan. 'Now that the weather has cleared, we can investigate the place where we saw Claudia as the Phantom. The mystery of the flashbulb will have to remain a mystery for the time being.'

'You won't find any clues there after all this rain,' Randall Scott cautioned.

'I suspect you are right, Randall,' agreed Susan. 'But we haven't been back to the falls since the storm came up. I am determined to discover how Claudia could play the Phantom and a short time later be sitting in a completely different spot with Mrs Tanner, eating her lunch.'

'A trip to the falls sounds fine to me,' said Brian, seating himself on one of the beds and removing his shoes. 'If we are going to take a hike, I'm putting on my trainers.'

'That's a good idea,' replied Susan. 'Marge and I will go back to the inn and get into our hiking clothes. We'll meet you in front of the inn in fifteen minutes.'

Soon the four friends were on their way to the Featherford Falls. When they reached the bridge that crossed Feather Creek, Susan stopped and contemplated the water as it rushed by on its journey from the falls.

'I would like to cross here and approach the falls from the other side,' she stated. 'When Claudia appeared, she was on the other side of this creek.'

'That's a sound deduction,' agreed Randall Scott. 'Maybe Claudia put on the Indian outfit somewhere over there in the woods, secretly made her way to the falls, emerged from the trees so you would all see her, and disappeared.'

'But disappeared where, Randall?' Susan asked. 'I have thought of the woods as the most reasonable place for Claudia to put on the Indian outfit, but how could she vanish so quickly?'

'If there were any footprints, they're all gone by now,' said Brian. 'The ground is still very wet.'

The quartet crossed the little bridge and made their way along the creek to the spot where Claudia had appeared as the Phantom.

'This area is completely in the open,' Susan noted. 'If Claudia came out of those woods over there, she would have to cross at least a hundred feet unprotected.'

'We would have seen her,' replied Marge. 'She seemed to come out of nowhere.'

The four scrutinised the ground around the falling water.

'Nothing but mud,' said Randall Scott.

'Let's take the path along the cliff to where I found Marge by the boulder,' suggested Susan, leading the way.

Slowly they climbed the narrow, winding track until they came to the boulder.

'I was lying behind that big rock,' said Marge, pointing.

'When I was hit on the head, I was standing just about where we are now. Whoever knocked me out must have dragged me back there.'

'Then they could only have been hiding behind those shrubs,' reasoned Professor Scott. 'There is absolutely no other place to be lurking unseen.'

'The rain has ruined any trace of footprints,' Susan moaned, her eyes scanning the ground.

The four walked over to the clump of shrubs, but the storm had obliterated any vestige of a clue. After searching the area thoroughly, they started back along the path. Halfway down the track, Susan stopped and looked up at the cliff, where the water ran down from its source and crashed over the rocks to fall in a thundering cascade. The side of the rocky wall was bare except for a thick line of small trees and untamed bushes and wild flowers which grew in profusion along the base of the cliff.

'I found the black feather just over there,' said Susan, indicating the spot on the other side of the path.

'Then Claudia Kingsley must have come along this track,' reasoned Brian.

'Unless the feather blew from another place,' Susan replied. 'Since she must have been running very fast, perhaps the feather flew out of her headband, was picked up by a breeze, and settled down where I found it.'

Still Susan stood by the cliff and studied the rocky surface.

'You're not contemplating the idea that Claudia scaled that cliff, are you, Sue?' asked Randall.

'No, that would be impossible, even for Brave Deer,' Susan returned, lowering her gaze. 'But I do have another idea that might be more plausible.'

The slim black-haired girl adjusted her glasses, walked over to a rugged projection of rocks covered with vines and shrubs, and began pulling them aside. For several minutes she groped and tugged until she had made her way through the heavy growth. The branches snapped back into place, and Susan was entirely hidden from view. Marge, Randall, and Brian, intrigued by her behaviour, approached the bushes and began to make their way through them.

'Sue, where are you?' cried Professor Scott as the trio emerged from the shrubbery and found themselves flattened up against the rocky wall.

'Where did she go?' cried Marge, turning her head to the right and left.

'She's disappeared!' exclaimed Brian, edging himself along the cliff.

'I'm in here!' called a muffled voice from a spot a dozen feet or so along the wall.

'Look, over there!' exclaimed Randall Scott. 'There's a small open area, where those big rocks are.'

The trio edged their way along the wall, over to the spot where Susan's voice seemed to be coming from.

'There's an opening in the cliff!' exclaimed Marge.

'So there is!' Brian said. 'But it's so small I doubt if we can get through.'

'You mean you doubt if *I* can get through,' retorted Marge. 'Brian Lorenzo, I am not that fat.'

Marge made her way to the hole and began to squeeze her way through, pushing her arms against the sides. She wriggled and twisted and puffed and, with a final push from Brian, stumbled into the blackness.

'Sue!' she called, but there was no answer.

'Why, it's a tunnel!' said Randall and Brian in unison as they squeezed their way through the opening.

'But where is Sue?' asked Marge. 'We don't have a torch, and it's dark in here.'

'Sue!' cried Randall Scott in a loud voice that echoed eerily down the narrow tunnel.

'She could only have come this way,' said Brian. 'But would she go into that blackness without a light?'

'She must have her torch,' replied Marge. 'Sue!'

'I'm going in there, light or no light,' Randall Scott

stated emphatically, starting at a rapid pace down the tunnel.

'Well, you're not leaving us behind,' said Marge, taking Brian's hand.

Feeling their way along the inky passageway, the trio went as fast as they dared. The floor of the tunnel was extremely uneven, and they stumbled many times.

'Sue!' called Randall Scott.

'I'm down here!' came a welcome voice.

At that moment a tiny spot of light could be seen ahead. The trio headed towards it eagerly and soon came upon Susan standing in a small alcove that jutted just off the tunnel.

'Sue, we were beginning to get worried about you,' cried Marge. 'I thought Randall might break a leg, running so fast over those rocks.'

'I have made an astounding discovery,' Susan Sand announced, flashing her torch around the little recess. 'This is where Claudia kept the Indian outfit and the suntan make-up that I noticed on her forehead. The costume has since been removed.'

'How can you be certain of that?' questioned Randall, placing an arm around her shoulder.

'I found this on the floor,' Susan replied, holding up a crumpled tissue and flashing the light on it. 'It's one of those pre-moistened towelettes, and it's covered with suntan make-up. Whoever came back for the Indian outfit and the wig overlooked this tissue.'

'Oh, Sue! You've solved it!' exclaimed Marge. 'This is where Claudia came to dress up as an Indian.'

'I think the tunnel goes all the way through to the other side,' Susan continued. 'Claudia must have come in here, got into the outfit, and then returned outside and appeared in front of us. Then she came back in here, removed the outfit and the make-up, and emerged from the cliff on the other side, where she joined Mrs "Tanner" in the field of wild flowers. Mrs "Tanner"

80

was lying when she said they had come from the inn.'

'Then let's push on and find the exit,' urged Randall Scott.

Excitedly the four friends continued on down the tunnel. In a very short time they came to an area where the passageway broadened, revealing a wall.

'The other side of the cliff!' Susan concluded.

'But where is the exit?' Brian asked.

Susan flashed her light over the wall until she found a spot where there was a recess. Walking over to it, she felt carefully but could find no opening.

'That's strange,' she mused. 'There was once an exit here, but it's all blocked up with boulders.'

'But your theory can't be wrong, Sue,' said Professor Scott. 'Claudia must have escaped this way.'

'There is no other exit here,' Susan stated, examining the entire expanse of wall. 'Only this spot, which is now sealed up with rocks. There must be another explanation.'

'I'm starting to get hungry,' announced Marge. 'As well as claustrophobic. My detective instincts end when my stomach is empty.'

'Let's return to where we came in and examine this wall from the outside,' Susan suggested.

As quickly as possible the quartet walked back down the tunnel to the entrance.

'Where is the hole?' asked Susan, flashing her light on the wall. 'I am certain it was just over there.'

'It was over there, Sue,' Randall Scott agreed, rushing to the spot.

Gravely he turned around and confronted the group. 'Our escape has been blocked up by a boulder,' he said, his voice tense.

'It can't be,' cried Susan, hurrying to his side and feeling the wall.

She turned to Marge, whose face was pale in the dim

light of the torch. Then she looked at Brian and Randall and leaned heavily against the wall.

'Someone has sealed us up in this tunnel,' she said, her eyes sombre. 'We've been imprisoned in here, and no one knows where we are!'

13

Up the wall

'We're trapped!' said Susan Sand.

'Who would do such a thing?' asked Marge.

'Perhaps we can move the boulder,' suggested Randall Scott. 'There's not much room for leverage, but if we all push hard, we might be able to dislodge it enough to squeeze out.'

Together the four friends pushed with all their strength on the boulder that blocked their way to freedom, but the huge stone did not move even a fraction of an inch.

'There must be other stones pushed up against this one,' said Brian Lorenzo.

'How are we going to get out?' Marge asked, her voice trembling.

'We'll try the other exit,' said Susan, starting down the tunnel. 'Perhaps we'll be lucky.'

Quietly the trio followed her down the twisting, narrow passageway, their progress lit by the dim beam of the torch, which Susan moved back and forth on the rocky ground.

'Everyone walk carefully,' advised Randall Scott. 'We don't need any sprained ankles.'

'I'm frightened,' announced Marge, holding onto Brian's hand. 'If we can't move the other boulder, we'll never get out. What will happen to us?'

'We are going to escape,' replied Susan emphatically. 'And we must not lose our heads.'

Silently the small group advanced down the tunnel. During their progress Susan studied the walls on each side, hoping to find some other means of exit that she had overlooked before.

'There are no other tunnels running off this main one,' she told herself, 'not even a tiny hole. Yet I can hear the sound of the falls as we move towards the other exit. It seems to be getting a bit louder.'

'Do you hear the sound of water?' she asked.

'Yes, and it is getting louder,' replied Professor Scott.

'Then there must be an opening somewhere,' reasoned Brian.

'Oh, where?' cried Marge. 'Yes, I hear water. Why didn't we notice the sound before?'

'Because we weren't listening for it,' answered Brian, squeezing her hand tightly.

By the time they reached the other end of the tunnel, the sound of rushing water had become even more pronounced.

'It seems to be coming from up there,' said Susan, pointing to a spot high up the tunnel wall to her right. 'Listen!'

Silently and expectantly the four friends looked up at the spot Susan indicated and strained to hear the rushing of the falling water as it ran over the cliff above their heads. Hopefully, Susan shone her light up along the wall.

'If there is a hole up there, I can't see it,' she said. 'This torch isn't powerful enough to reach all the way to the ceiling.'

'But there is an opening, or we couldn't hear the noise of the water so clearly,' replied Randall.

'Let's try pushing on this boulder,' said Brian, applying his shoulder to the stone. 'We might be able to move it.'

Together the friends tried to dislodge the big rock but were no more successful than on their first try at the other end of the tunnel.

'I'm just going to have to scale that wall and find out where the opening is,' announced Susan Sand.

'Susan!' exclaimed Professor Scott. 'That's a sure way to break your neck. And even if there is a hole, it might not be big enough to get through.'

'Nevertheless, I must try,' Susan insisted. 'The wall is very uneven, and there are many places to hold on to. I think I can use the projections like a stairway.'

'If you insist on being so foolhardy, then I will just have to join you,' replied Randall Scott.

'I'll go first,' Susan said, placing a foot on a rock and pulling herself up. 'The torch goes in my pocket, and I don't intend to look back.'

Marge Halloran was close to tears as she stood and watched her friend begin the ascent up the wall.

'At least we wore trainers,' said Brian consolingly. 'And Susan is extremely agile.'

'It's a good thing that Professor Scott plays football and keeps in good condition,' added Marge.

Slowly the pair made their way up the rocky wall. Inch by inch they moved closer to the ceiling, gripping each rocky projection with their rubber-soled trainers. Neither Brian nor Marge moved or made a sound as they stood tensely with their heads back, watching.

'There's a ledge here, Randall,' Susan called out. 'It's wide enough to sit on and rest.'

'Wonderful!' he replied. 'Save a place for me.'

Several minutes later Susan and Randall had scrambled onto a wide piece of rock that jutted out several feet from the wall. Carefully Susan removed the torch from her pocket and shone it up towards the ceiling.

'Randall, there *is* a hole. Look! It's quite large.'

'So there is.' He whistled. 'I see daylight.'

'Hey, what are you two talking about?' cried Brian. 'You're keeping us in suspense.'

'We see a pretty big hole,' Randall Scott returned. 'It looks as if Susan might be able to get through it.'

'Hurray!' cried the pair on the ground.

'Please don't rush,' cautioned Marge.

Carefully the two climbers rose from their perch and started a snail-like ascent towards the opening.

'If I fall, Randall, I will certainly hit you,' said Susan. 'I think it would be wiser if you remained on the ledge while I try to reach the opening.'

'I'm staying right behind you,' he answered decisively. 'If you fall, then I will fall too.'

Judiciously Susan edged her way towards the opening. She moved so slowly and deliberately that Brian and Marge could only marvel at her sense of balance and sure footing.

'Sue certainly can keep her head,' whispered Marge, biting her lower lip. 'I could never do that in a million years.'

As soon as Susan Sand reached the edge of the hole, she grasped it firmly with both hands and relaxed for a moment, resting her tired body against the wall. For several moments she remained motionless. Then, with one graceful movement, she pulled herself through the opening.

'She made it!' cried Marge.

'Sssh!' said Brian, placing a hand on her mouth. 'You'll disturb Professor Scott. He has to reach the hole too.'

Slowly the young professor made his way towards the aperture. He moved with great ease and steadiness and soon was grasping the edge of the hole and pulling himself through to freedom.

'There is a very wide ledge here,' said Susan as she helped him onto the stony projection. 'Do you know where we are? In the cavern behind the falls.'

Professor Scott looked down from the rocky perch and drew in his breath. They were high up in the wide cavern. Behind and on both sides there was nothing but sheer wall, glistening with dampness. In front, the water from the falls cascaded over the opening.

'There is no way we can possibly reach the ground,' said the young man, holding Susan firmly around the waist.

'Randall, we are trapped up here,' Susan replied. 'There is no place where we could get a foothold. What are we to do?'

14

Wolf Dog acts

'We must escape,' Susan Sand declared resolutely. 'But how are we to descend a sheer, slippery wall?'

'It looks impossible,' Randall Scott replied. 'Yet there is no sense in climbing back through the hole. There is no exit from the tunnel. We're trapped either way.'

'How frustrating!' exclaimed Susan. 'If only we could sprout wings!'

'Hey, you two,' called Brian. 'Are you still there?'

Carefully Randall Scott turned around and thrust his head through the hole. 'We can't get to the ground,' he explained. 'We're perched up here like two baby birds that haven't learned to fly.'

'Perhaps if you shout loud enough, someone outside will hear you,' yelled Brian.

'There seems to be no other choice,' Randall Scott agreed, pulling his head back through the opening.

Together Susan and Randall shouted for help until their voices began to become hoarse.

'No one is around,' said Susan. 'It's getting late in the day. Randall, I don't think we have much of a chance of being discovered until tomorrow.'

At that moment the raven-haired girl adjusted her glasses and looked over to where the water cascaded in front of the cavern.

'Randall, there's Icky! Over on the other side of the falls! He must have followed us earlier and just now heard us calling.'

'I have never known a cat that would go for help,' the

professor answered in a dry tone. 'I'm afraid, Sue, Icky won't be much help to us.'

'No, he won't. But look who is with him.'

'Wolf Dog!' cried Randall Scott. 'She's been playing with Icky.'

'Wolf Dog!' the two cried in unison. 'Wolf Dog, come here!'

The big animal turned her head at the sound of her name and started towards the cavern at a fast trot.

'She is used to this cave,' said Susan. 'Brave Deer came here all the time until the Phantom frightened him away.'

In no time Wolf Dog had entered the cavern and stood rigidly beneath the pair, barking shrilly.

'Wolf Dog, go for Brave Deer,' Susan commanded. 'Go find Brave Deer!'

Momentarily the beautiful animal looked up, her head cocked to one side. Then she turned around and ran swiftly out of the cavern and disappeared around the corner of the cliff.

'She'll bring him back. I know she will,' Susan cried.

Anxiously the pair waited on the ledge, but their impatience was short-lived. Within a short time, Wolf Dog reappeared with Brave Deer.

'How did you get up there?' the Indian boy called to them. 'Don't tell me you found the tunnel and climbed up the wall!'

'That's exactly what we did,' cried Susan. 'How do you know about the tunnel and the hole?'

'I discovered it when I was very small,' he replied. 'Why did you do such a dangerous thing as to scale the wall?'

'Someone trapped us in the tunnel, Brave Deer,' Susan explained. 'They rolled boulders in front of both entrances. Our friends, Marge Halloran and Brian Lorenzo, are still inside.'

'Trapped you in the tunnel!' Brave Deer exclaimed. 'Who would do such a terrible thing?'

'We don't know,' answered Susan. 'Can you get us down?'

'Yes. It is no problem,' the boy answered. 'I will go and get my uncle, Black Cloud. He has a rope ladder.'

Brave Deer turned and ran from the cavern, Wolf Dog trotting alongside, barking with excitement.

'That dog deserves a medal,' said Randall Scott.

'I think Icky deserves one too, for just being outside,' returned Susan defensively. 'After all, if Ikhnaton hadn't followed us, Wolf Dog wouldn't have been there to save us.'

'That's what I call deductive reasoning,' Professor Scott teased. 'There is a great deal of logic in it.'

Susan Sand laughed good-naturedly and then made her way to the opening and called the good news to Brian and Marge.

'Hooray!' they cried.

'Now we can eat lunch,' added Marge.

Within ten minutes, Brave Deer and Black Cloud ran into the cave. The older Indian was carrying a rolled-up rope ladder.

'We will release your friends from the tunnel as soon as you are safely on the ground,' said Black Cloud, unfolding the rope ladder. 'I will throw this up to you. You must fasten it securely on that projection to your left. I am afraid that the ladder will not reach all the way to the ground, but we will be able to help you the last part of the way.'

Black Cloud threw back his arm and with a powerful thrust flung the ladder up towards Susan and Randall, who reached over the edge of the ledge as far as was safely possible. The first two times the ladder fell to the ground, but on the third try Susan was able to grasp one end of it.

'Good catch!' cried Brave Deer.

Randall and Susan tied the ends of the ladder tightly around a rocky projection and tested it before chancing the descent.

'I'll try it, Sue,' said the professor. 'If it will hold me, it will hold you.'

With all his considerable strength, Randall Scott tugged on the ladder. When he was certain that it would hold, he turned around and began to descend. The ladder rested against the damp wall and felt relatively stable as the young man climbed carefully to the floor of the cavern. Susan quickly followed.

'We can never thank you enough,' she said to the two Indians as they lifted her the last few feet to the ground. 'But how will you retrieve your ladder, Black Cloud?'

'I will climb the tunnel wall and untie it,' said Brave Deer. 'Now we must release your friends.'

'Wolf Dog, without you, we would have been up there for a very long time,' said Susan, placing her arms around the big animal's neck and kissing her on the top of the head. Wolf Dog licked Susan's face with her large pink tongue and then barked jubilantly.

'Come, we will roll the boulders away from the exit where your friends are waiting,' said Black Cloud, turning towards the cave opening. 'Then we must find out who did this terrible thing.'

Quickly they left the cave and ran around the side of the cliff to the nearest exit, which was the opposite one from where they had entered. Two large boulders blocked the opening, and several smaller ones were pushed up against them.

'Brian was right,' said Susan. 'Whoever trapped us in the tunnel wanted to make certain we didn't escape.'

'What a chance they took,' commented Randall Scott. 'There is no thick shrubbery covering up this opening. They might easily have been seen.'

'It could have been one person,' said Susan, 'but only a strong man would be able to move these stones alone.'

Together the two Indians rolled the boulders aside, and Marge and Brian rushed from the tunnel, the redhead throwing her arms around Black Cloud and kissing him on the cheek. The Indian seemed embarrassed and murmured something about how glad he was that he could be of help.

'We might have starved to death in there!' exclaimed Marge.

'Look, there's Icky,' said Brian as the marmalade cat emerged from the woods. 'Just like a cat to appear when all the danger is over!'

'You must come to my cabin,' Black Cloud said, his voice very commanding. 'You are exhausted and hungry, and the sun is almost down. There is food for the cat also.'

'Black Cloud, we couldn't intrude on you,' replied Susan. 'The inn is not far.'

'No, you must come to my cabin,' he insisted. 'It is a short distance from here. I want to talk to you about this.'

'Very well, Black Cloud,' Susan replied, picking up Icky. 'I am sure we would all be grateful for a rest and some food.'

Silently the little group followed Black Cloud through the thick woods and soon came upon a large log cabin. It rested in a small clearing and seemed very inviting to the weary friends. Courteously the Indian escorted them inside.

'How charming!' said Marge, looking around the airy, simply furnished living-room.

'Did you make that fieldstone fireplace, Black Cloud?' asked Brian.

'Yes,' the Indian replied. 'I built the entire cabin. Please be seated. I will make us some supper. Come, Brave Deer, you help me.'

'This is more fun than the Waldorf,' said Marge in a whisper after the Indians had disappeared into the next room. 'How nice of Black Cloud to ask us here.'

'Black Cloud is no fool,' returned Susan, smiling. 'He's not going to let us go until we tell him what happened.'

15

Revelations

'That was a wonderful meal, Black Cloud,' Susan Sand said. 'You are a first-rate chef.'

'I am not used to cooking for so many people,' the Indian replied, smiling slightly. 'It is an occasion to have you all as guests.'

'Look at Wolf Dog stretched out in front of the fireplace with Icky between her paws,' commented Marge. 'They act as if they had known each other for years.'

'Wolf Dog had a litter of puppies not long ago,' explained Brave Deer. 'When we gave them away, she missed them. She is enjoying mothering your cat, Miss Sand.'

'I have never seen Ikhnaton more contented,' replied Susan.

'It is better than being chased up a tree,' responded Brave Deer, laughing.

Outside, the sun had set and the blackness of the forest surrounded the cabin. Several windows were open, and strange sounds of nocturnal animals disturbed the silence. A gentle, warm breeze blew softly through the room, bringing with it the scent of pine trees and wet earth.

'I feel very cut off from the world,' said Susan Sand. 'You must live a peaceful life here, Black Cloud.'

The Indian rose from the table and walked over to one of the windows, pulling a pipe from a pocket and lighting it.

'Miss Sand, what you say is true,' he answered. 'That is, until recently.'

'What do you mean, Black Cloud?' Susan asked, turning in her chair.

'I am going to answer your question by asking you one,' he replied, looking out the window, his sharp profile silhouetted against the pane. 'Why were you in the tunnel behind the falls?'

'The question requires a complicated answer, Black Cloud,' she replied, glancing across the table at Randall Scott.

'Perhaps I can answer part of it for you,' the Indian said, puffing on his pipe. 'You were trying to discover who was frightening my nephew by dressing up as an Odega and appearing in front of the falls.'

'How do you know that?' Marge blurted.

'My uncle and I had a long talk this afternoon,' explained Brave Deer, rising from the table and crossing over to where Wolf Dog and Icky lay. He sat down on the floor cross-legged and stroked the big animal's head. 'I know now that I did not see a phantom but a flesh-and-blood person.'

'Someone is victimising my nephew,' exclaimed Black Cloud, his face taut with anger. 'Who would do such a thing to him, and who would trap you people in the tunnel? Certainly the two episodes are connected.'

'Yes, Black Cloud, they are,' Susan answered, getting up from her chair and looking at the older Indian. 'I think it is time that we were frank with each other.'

Susan walked over to a small table and picked up her purse, withdrawing from it a long envelope. From the envelope she took out the black feather and held it up.

'Saturday I found this feather near the tunnel entrance on the other side of the falls,' she explained. 'That same afternoon, when you came to my room at the inn, Black Cloud, you wanted to talk to me until you saw it lying on the bureau. At the time, Marge and I were baffled as to why the sight of a feather could make you change so completely.'

'Then you have learned that that black feather from a species of hawk no longer in this area means cowardice to us Odegas,' said Brave Deer, rising to his feet.

'Yes, Brave Deer,' Susan replied quietly. 'Rose Petal told us the meaning of the feather and the story of White Rabbit. We realised that the feather had been stolen from the museum. I have not yet said anything to Rose Petal about finding it, because it is such a valuable clue. The "Phantom" wore the feather in its headband.'

'I thought I was seeing the ghost of White Rabbit through the falling water,' said Brave Deer gravely. 'He was the brother of an ancestor of mine. I became afraid to go near the falls.'

'Can you think of any explanation for someone wanting to keep you away from the falls?' asked Brian.

'No, it is ridiculous!' the young Indian exclaimed. 'It seems completely senseless.'

'According to Farmer Smythe, White Rabbit was not a coward,' said Susan.

Briefly she told the two Indians of the diary that belonged to Irongate University and of the reference to White Rabbit.

'The diary is a valuable document to you Odegas,' said Professor Scott. 'I will try to get the university to return it to you.'

'That part of our history is shrouded in mystery,' commented Black Cloud, staring out the window into the night. 'Always people have said that White Rabbit was a coward because the Pipe of Peace was never found and the boy disappeared. Now we have evidence that that may not be so.'

'We made another important discovery,' Susan continued. 'Since the rain had stopped, we decided to investigate the area where we saw the "Phantom", and we found the tunnel entrance. Inside, we came upon this lying in an alcove halfway through the passageway.'

Susan pulled the piece of tissue stained with suntan make-up from her pocket and showed it to the two Indians.

'But who would do this to me?' cried Brave Deer, fingering the tissue.

'Brave Deer, we have discovered who the "Phantom" is,' Susan announced, her voice gentle. 'You must understand that it was done out of fear. Brave Deer, Claudia Kingsley is the person who played the "Phantom".'

'Claudia!' the boy exclaimed, a shocked expression on his face.

'She has been terrified,' Randall Scott interjected, going to the Indian and placing a hand on his shoulder.

'That is why she nearly fainted in the dining-room when she dropped the tray of dishes,' added Marge. 'She didn't want to do it, Brave Deer, but someone made her.'

'Claudia!' the boy repeated in a hoarse voice. 'How could anyone make her do that to me? She has been my friend since we were little.'

'Miss Sand and the professor are right,' Black Cloud stated. 'Claudia would never do such a thing on her own. Have you spoken to the girl, Miss Sand?'

'No, Black Cloud,' she replied. 'We have not wanted to show our hand. There is too much behind this to take any rash steps.'

'You are wise,' said Black Cloud, his face grim. 'How can you be certain that Claudia is the one who played the "Phantom"?'

Susan related to the Indians how she had seen suntan make-up around Claudia's hairline shortly after the 'Phantom' had appeared at the falls.

'Also, Marge thought she recognised Claudia behind the disguise, and she followed her,' continued Susan. 'Then someone hit Marge on the head and dragged her behind a big boulder.'

'Then we are dealing with desperate people!' exclaimed the older Indian. 'You did not see who hit you, Miss Halloran?'

'No, Black Cloud,' the redhead answered. 'I just felt that the "Phantom" was Claudia when she appeared through the falling water, and I ran from the cave and up the path, but she had disappeared. Now I know that she escaped into the tunnel.'

'It is most likely that the same person or persons who hit you also trapped you in the tunnel,' Black Cloud concluded.

'That seems to be the most reasonable explanation,' Susan agreed.

Black Cloud paced back and forth in front of the window, puffing on his pipe, his face stern. After several minutes he stopped and turned to the four friends.

'There is something that I must tell you,' he began. 'There is only one person to whom I have spoken about this – Mrs Vandervelden. I confided in her last spring when the robberies started.'

'Robberies!' the group exclaimed.

'Yes. Several wealthy guests at the inn have been robbed while they were on camping trips with me. Always their apartments in New York City were broken into. Nothing was ever taken at the inn.'

'These must be the same robberies Mrs Vandervelden and her friend, Mrs Minton, told us about, Marge,' said Susan Sand, adjusting her glasses.

'Mrs Vandervelden spoke to you?' Black Cloud asked, raising his eyebrows.

'Yes, Black Cloud,' Susan answered. 'But she said nothing about you. At the time I wondered why she was telling me about them, since there didn't seem to be any relation between the robberies and the mystery of the falls.'

'I do not know if the two are connected,' the older Indian commented. 'But I do know that someone is trying to place the blame for the robberies on me!'

'On you!' cried Susan. 'But that's absurd!'

Black Cloud laughed grimly. 'Since I am responsible for the camping trips, some people concluded that I must be guilty of the robberies, even though I was off in the woods at the time they occurred,' he responded. 'One policeman intimated that I was the head of a gang and was clever enough to be elsewhere during the thefts.'

'Black Cloud, how dreadful!' cried Marge.

'I spoke to Mrs Vandervelden because she is a good friend and she knows that I am incapable of such a scheme,' the Indian added. 'I felt that I had to confide in someone, since my reputation is at stake. And now this "Phantom" appears at the falls and frightens Brave Deer into thinking that he is seeing the ghost of White Rabbit. Do you not see why I think there is a conspiracy against us?'

'Yes, Black Cloud, I can understand your concern,' said Susan. 'Now I realise that Mrs Vandervelden was trying to gain my assistance without implicating you.'

'She is a loyal friend,' Black Cloud replied.

'What are we to do?' Brave Deer asked. 'Perhaps if I talk to Claudia, she will tell me who is making her play the "Phantom".'

'No, Brave Deer,' Susan cautioned. 'We mustn't show the culprit or culprits that we have unmasked the "Phantom". There is still a great deal of investigation to be done. We need evidence, and we have to find out if there is a connection between the robberies and the "Phantom".'

'I saw you running away from the inn on Friday night, Black Cloud,' Marge stammered. 'We couldn't imagine why you were there, when a camping party had left just that morning. We actually suspected you of something.'

'I have been playing detective,' the Indian replied, laughing heartily. 'But I am not doing so well, if you saw me.'

'Everything is becoming more clear,' said Susan. 'We did suspect you, Black Cloud, when we saw you again, talking to Barry Hearne Saturday night during that pouring rain.'

Black Cloud laughed again. 'I can see that you are very good detectives. Mr Hearne approached me when I was on my way here to my cabin. He pulled me aside and asked me when the next camping trip would be.'

'I knew that fellow was up to no good!' exclaimed Randall Scott. 'He's been following Susan around, even to the point of trailing her to Thornewood when she came to see me.'

'I do not know what to make of Mr Hearne,' said Black Cloud, almost to himself. 'He has been very nosy and shows up in the most unexpected places. Yet he is likable.'

'He has a certain charm,' agreed Susan. 'But charm is deceiving.'

'You can say that again,' Professor Scott interjected. 'He wanted to give Susan an Indian blanket when she barely knows him. Now it's beginning to look as if he is the head of a gang.'

'Please, Randall,' said Susan, somewhat embarrassed. 'We have no evidence against Barry Hearne. There are other suspects. Our task is to sort them out and arrive at the truth.'

16

Another mystery solved

After thanking Black Cloud profusely for his hospitality and promising to keep him informed of developments, the four friends returned to the inn. Brave Deer remained behind with his uncle, saying he would join them at the inn later.

As Susan entered the lobby, she was delighted to find a message waiting for her from Chief Burton of the Thornewood Police Department. The clerk at the desk handed her a piece of paper with a telephone number on it. Quickly she found a phone booth and dialled the number.

'Chief Burton,' said an authoritative voice on the other end of the wire.

'Chief, this is Susan Sand. I just this minute got back to the inn. Do you have some information for me?'

'Yes,' he replied. 'The "Tanners" have a record. They served time in Arizona for posing as geologists named Windom and robbing apartments while the guests were off on skiing holidays. The descriptions fit those you gave me of the "Tanners". Apparently they followed the same pattern. They went to a well-known ski lodge, somehow got hold of keys belonging to wealthy guests, and robbed their apartments in the city while those guests were on skiing jaunts.'

'They must be the same people!' Susan exclaimed, her voice low. 'Are they being sought by the police now?'

'No. They served their time, and at the moment there is nothing new against them.'

'Then I must get proof that they are doing the same thing here at the Feather Inn.'

'You should go to the local police, Susan,' Chief Burton advised. 'These people are experienced criminals. There is no telling what they might try next if they think you are on to them.'

'You are right,' replied Susan, but she did not reveal that that very day the four friends had been trapped in the tunnel. 'The problem is not Chief Burton's,' Susan told herself. 'So I will not worry him.'

'Susan, are you still there?' asked the chief.

'Yes, Chief. I was thinking about my next step. I can't thank you enough for this information.'

'You be careful,' he warned. 'And let me know of your progress.'

Susan thanked him again and hung up. Marge, Brian, and Randall were waiting for her in the lounge, but Susan refused to say anything to them until they were all safely in her room. Marge, who had been carrying Icky, placed him on the bed and flopped down next to him.

Jubilantly Susan related her conversation with Chief Burton.

'They certainly sound like the same people,' Professor Scott commented. 'But how do they get hold of the keys to those apartments in the city?'

'They must have a master key to the doors in the inn,' reasoned Brian.

'And when the people are off on camping trips they go into their rooms, take the keys, and go to the city and rob the apartments,' Marge deduced.

'That all makes sense, except for one thing,' said Susan Sand, her eyes narrowing. 'They would have to return the keys, or the guests would miss them as soon as they came back to their rooms.'

'Yes, that's reasonable,' agreed Randall Scott. 'Still, the "Tanners" could get back into the rooms if they have a master key. But they would be taking a chance.'

'I have it,' exclaimed Susan, her green eyes sparkling. 'The wax!'

'What wax?' Brian asked.

'The wax on Icky's foot, silly!' chided Marge in a teasing manner. 'Remember, we told you that last Friday night, when we returned late to the inn, we saw Barry Hearne in the hall picking at Icky's foot? Well, he was trying to get wax out of his fur. Somehow Icky had stepped in soft wax and was shaking his foot in an attempt to get it off.'

'You're right, Sue,' Brian cried. 'They must take wax impressions of the keys.'

'In that case, they would not have to steal the keys,' Randall Scott added.

'I must get into the "Tanners'" room,' said Susan. 'Finding the wax would be solid evidence against them.'

'Sue, you begin to worry me when you get that expression on your face,' said Professor Scott. 'You could go to jail for breaking and entering.'

'Not if I posed as a maid and got into their room with a key,' she rejoined.

'Where are you going to get a key to their room?' he asked.

'From Brave Deer,' she answered. 'I am certain he would be willing to assist us. His reputation and that of Black Cloud are at stake. I am going to find him right now. We can make our plans tonight. Brave Deer knows the routine of the inn. He could tell me when would be the best time to enter the "Tanners'" room, and he can get me a maid's uniform.'

Without further comment, Susan rushed from the room and returned five minutes later with Brave Deer and Wolf Dog. As soon as she had closed the door she related to Brave Deer her conversation with Chief Burton and her plans for getting into the 'Tanners'' room.

'Of course I will help,' the boy replied calmly. 'That is a clever scheme. The maids finish on the second floor,

101

where the "Tanners'" room is, by eleven o'clock in the morning. I can easily get you a maid's uniform. Wolf Dog and I will remain on guard outside to make certain no one catches you.'

'I don't like it, Sue,' Randall Scott announced, pacing the floor. 'We are dealing with desperate people. They are hardened criminals.'

'They certainly don't act like hardened criminals. They go around collecting flowers and taking pictures,' said Marge.

'A very skilful cover-up,' Brian replied.

'What worries me is Mr Kingsley,' said Professor Scott. 'What if he is in with the "Tanners"? Even if they are off collecting flowers, he might come to the second floor for some reason and see you. Besides him, there is that Barry Hearne. He is so interested in you he follows you around all the time.'

'No matter,' Susan insisted. 'I must get into that room, and I intend to do it tomorrow morning.'

By eleven-thirty the following morning, Susan was prepared for her adventure. Brave Deer had found her a uniform that fitted her quite well, and a matching head-piece so she could conceal her very noticeable raven hair. He had seen the 'Tanners' leave the inn an hour before.

'I don't need my glasses,' she decided. 'What I'm looking for is a cake of wax. It shouldn't be hard to find.'

'What if they have locked it up — say, in a suitcase?' asked Randall Scott.

'I'll face that problem if and when I come to it,' she replied. 'Now you all stay out of sight here in my room. Brave Deer and Wolf Dog are the only ones who can loiter around in the halls and not be suspected.'

'I have told Wolf Dog to bark two times if I give her the signal,' Brave Deer said. 'If I see anyone coming along who might go into the "Tanners'" room, I will raise my arm and she will bark to warn you.'

'How clever you are, Wolf Dog!' Marge exclaimed. 'You saved our lives, and now you are being a detective.'

Apprehensively, the four friends watched as Susan slipped from her room after Brave Deer had made certain no one was in the hall. He sauntered casually down the hall with Wolf Dog, and Susan followed. When they had reached the second floor, Brave Deer opened the door of a linen closet and pretended to be fixing the lock. Quickly Susan drew the key that he had given her from a pocket and let herself into the 'Tanners'' room.

Rapidly Susan looked around to get her bearings. Several suitcases stood in one corner, and she immediately went over to them and found that they were locked.

'I'll worry about them later,' she told herself.

Swiftly and deftly she opened drawers and rifled through clothing and other personal belongings. Each drawer was carefully searched, but nothing suspicious was found. Susan looked everywhere, including the back of the portable radio, but there was no sign of any wax. Even the mattress was thoroughly examined.

'I have exhausted this room,' she said to herself ruefully. 'There is only the bathroom.'

Before she entered that room, she placed her ear against the door to the hall but could hear nothing. 'The inn is certainly deserted at this hour on a beautiful summer day,' she thought. 'Now for the bathroom!'

There was one small cabinet over the sink, and a wastebasket, which was empty. Opening the door of the cabinet, Susan began to look through the items that lined the shelves.

'Toothpaste, mouthwash, razor blades, antacid, aspirin, soap,' said Susan. 'Everything one would expect to find in a bathroom. But no wax!'

Every item in the cabinet was examined, but there was nothing at all suspicious. Just as Susan was about to give up in disgust, she picked up the box that held the cake of soap and studied it again.

'This is one of those expensive, scented bars that no hotel would ever give to their guests,' Susan said to herself. 'Mrs Tanner must have brought it with her.'

Susan opened the box, and a square cake slipped into her hand.

'This isn't soap,' she said jubilantly. 'It's a cake of wax! The paper wrapping is from a dental-supply house.'

At that moment Susan heard two shrill barks. 'Someone is coming!' she thought in dismay.

Putting the wax back into the box, she replaced it on the shelf and closed the cabinet door.

Again two loud barks sounded in the hall.

'I must get out of here!' she said in a panic and rushed to the door.

17

Fawn Rock

Carefully Susan Sand opened the door to the hall and peeked out. Mr 'Tanner' had just reached the top of the stairs and had turned to start down the hall, but Brave Deer stopped him and held him in conversation. Quickly Susan slipped through the door into the hall and walked rapidly in the other direction. Wolf Dog, who had been posted near the back staircase, wagged her tail as Susan hurried by.

'Thank you, Wolf Dog,' she whispered as she started up the staircase to the third floor. 'You are a first-rate lookout.'

Wolf Dog wagged her tail vigorously but remained silent and trotted off down the corridor to join Brave Deer.

When Susan reached her room, she excitedly told Marge, Brian, and Randall Scott of her discovery of the wax in the 'Tanners'' bathroom.

'It's dental wax,' she explained. 'The kind dentists use to take impressions.'

'Perfect for making impressions of keys,' commented Professor Scott.

'Did Mr "Tanner" see you, Sue?' asked Marge excitedly.

'I don't know, but he certainly looked in my direction,' she answered. 'Another second or so, and he would have caught me.'

There was a knock on the door and as Susan called, 'Come in!' Brave Deer and Wolf Dog entered.

'He saw you!' the Indian exclaimed. 'I don't think he

recognised you, but he asked me why a maid should be leaving his room at that hour. He might be suspicious. It's my fault for not giving Wolf Dog the signal sooner, but Mr "Tanner" came into the lobby and up the stairs so fast, he caught me off guard.'

'It was worth it, Brave Deer,' said Susan. 'I found the wax. You did splendidly, and so did you, Wolf Dog. Even if. Mr "Tanner" saw me leave, he couldn't possibly recognise me at that distance and with my hair up and my glasses off.'

'I hope you are right, Sue,' replied Randall Scott, a worried expression on his rugged features. 'When you are dealing with people like the "Tanners", caution is the best policy.'

'If I were cautious, I would never solve anything,' Susan reminded him. 'Now we know for certain that the "Tanners" are responsible for the thefts that have occurred since last spring.'

'Even though you found the wax, Sue, it still isn't proof that the "Tanners" are the culprits,' said Brian. 'If only they could be caught red-handed!'

'Mr "Tanner" is going to be more careful than ever,' offered Randall Scott.

'We must devise a scheme to catch them doing their dirty work,' resolved Susan.

'How can you do that?' asked Brave Deer.

'I think your uncle will help, Brave Deer,' Susan replied. 'We must plan a camping trip and trap the "Tanners" into pulling off another theft.'

'But would they fall for it, Sue?' Professor Scott asked.

'I think they will if it's done cleverly,' the black-haired girl replied. 'Before we talk to Black Cloud about it, however, I want to get into that storage room in Farmer Smythe's house.'

'You mean because you saw the flashbulb there,' said Marge.

'Yes. I think Mrs "Tanner" was in that room taking

106

pictures,' Susan revealed. 'She always walks around with her camera. It's one of her props. It seems to me she is the most likely person to have left that flashbulb behind.'

'Barry Hearne also stayed in that room,' Randall Scott reminded her.

'Whoever dropped that bulb, we must get into the room and investigate,' stated Susan Sand.

'Sue, the door to the storage room is locked, and I returned the key of our room to Mr Kingsley this morning. He has a vacancy here in the inn, and we are moving today,' Randall informed her.

'I can get in through the window,' replied Susan determinedly. 'But not until tonight. I just hope that Mr Kingsley isn't giving the room to someone else.'

'Unfortunately I do not have a key to Smythe House,' said Brave Deer. 'Getting in through the window is a good idea, but you must let me do it.'

'No, Brave Deer,' Susan replied. 'Your reputation is too important to you and to your uncle. It would be too dangerous. I am used to detective work. I will go to the farmhouse alone and investigate that room.'

'You will not go alone unless I am chained to the wall,' retorted Randall Scott.

'But Randall, two people would attract more attention,' Susan countered.

'The professor is right,' offered Brave Deer. 'You need a lookout, just like today.'

'Yes, you are right,' Susan relented. 'We will go tonight to the Smythe farmhouse, Randall.'

'Meanwhile, since it is such a beautiful day, how are we going to while away the time?' Brian asked.

'I have not wanted to say anything,' replied Brave Deer unexpectedly, 'but early this morning at dawn I went to the falls. I wanted to see if I could discover the reason for someone trying to keep me away from there.'

'And what did you find out?' Marge asked.

'I cannot tell you here,' the Indian replied. 'You must

all come with me to the falls, and I will show you something very strange.'

'What do you mean, "strange", Brave Deer?' Susan asked, brushing a strand of hair from her forehead.

'I will not say anything until we have reached the falls,' the boy insisted.

Brave Deer remained adamant and would not say a word to the four friends. He said that before he showed them his discovery, he wanted to get Black Cloud and bring him to the falls with them. Half an hour later, the group started out on the journey, Brave Deer and Wolf Dog in the lead. When they reached the falls, the boy ran off into the woods towards his uncle's cabin, saying he would return within a short time with his uncle.

'Why is he so mysterious?' asked Marge, her face flushed with excitement. 'I never saw him act like this.'

'He must have made a significant discovery,' Susan concluded. 'We must be patient and let Brave Deer tell us in his own way.'

'What a beautiful sight,' commented Brian, looking up at the breathtaking vista of clear, sparkling water cascading hundreds of feet to the pool below. 'I have never seen anything like it.'

'Brave Deer understands this spot like no one else,' said Susan. 'He has a feeling for it that we can't approach. It's a respect and a reverence for nature which his ancestors experienced many centuries ago.'

'I think I can sense a part of what Brave Deer must feel,' commented Professor Scott. 'I envy his rapport with creation. We have indeed lost a great deal.'

Soon Brave Deer returned, followed by his uncle. Black Cloud strode purposefully towards the group, his face stern. He greeted them cordially, but his demeanour was such that conversation seemed inappropriate, and they walked silently behind Brave Deer towards the cavern. Susan sensed that the boy had told his uncle about the wax, but she said nothing.

Carefully the Indian boy picked his way over the slippery rocks and led them behind the falling water to the spot where they had observed the 'Phantom'. Brave Deer leaned forward and stared out through the rainbow of colours, which seemed all the more spectacular, for the sun was at its zenith. The brightness caused the water to reflect every colour of the spectrum.

'It's gorgeous!' whispered Marge, following Brave Deer's example by leaning forward and observing the view from his perspective.

'I want you all to look across the valley at the mountain on the other side,' he advised them. 'You must look from the exact spot where I am now standing. After you have studied the mountain, tell me what you saw.'

Each person in turn intently scanned the panorama across the lush valley. The mountain rose majestically and was covered with the varicoloured greens of the summer foliage. High up on the side of the cliff was a huge rock formation that stood out in marked contrast to the trees that grew on either side. When Susan's turn came, she adjusted her glasses several times and peered out at the mountain, her lithe body tense.

'There is a shape to that big rock that seems to represent something, Brave Deer,' she said, looking earnestly at the boy.

Wolf Dog stared up at Susan, her intelligent face expectant.

'Wolf Dog knows that you have sensed something,' said Brave Deer. 'You are beginning to see what I want you to see. Please look again, especially at the centre of the rock.'

Susan did as the Indian suggested. After studying the rock formation for several minutes, she drew back, smiling.

'What did you see?' asked Brave Deer.

'May I keep that to myself until my friends have had another turn?' she replied. 'I would like them to make a judgement also.'

'Of course,' Brave Deer answered.

In turn, Marge, Brian, and Randall Scott stood and looked again at the rock formation, each taking time to scan the entire mountain and its surrounding forest.

'I, too, would like to look again,' said Black Cloud. 'Although I know what Brave Deer has discovered, I want to see for myself.'

The older Indian stepped to the spot and bent his powerful form forward. He remained completely motionless for so long that Susan wondered if he had turned to stone. Suddenly he turned about, his black eyes gleaming, and looked at his nephew.

'You saw it, Uncle?' the boy asked.

'Yes, you are right. It is indeed changed.'

'What is changed?' squealed Marge, her patience giving way to her curiosity.

'What did you see when you looked out?' Brave Deer asked.

'I saw the outline of an animal's foot,' replied Susan. 'What did you see, Randall?'

'To me, it looked like a long snout, or maybe a tail,' he answered.

'I saw something that might be an arrow,' offered Brian. 'It is bent, but it comes to a point.'

'I agree with Susan,' said Marge. 'The rock looks like an animal's hoof.'

'You and Miss Sand are correct,' replied Brave Deer. 'What we have all been observing through the falling water is Fawn Rock. The projection on the right side of the mountain is in the shape of a fawn's hoof, raised in flight, as if it is running very fast. Fawn Rock has been known to us Odegas for hundreds of years.'

'What did you mean, Black Cloud, when you said it is changed?' Susan asked expectantly.

'The fawn's hoof has dropped somewhat,' he replied, turning to his nephew. 'Is that not so, Nephew?'

'Yes, Uncle,' the boy responded, his face grave. 'In

110

some incredible way Fawn Rock has moved its position. The change is so slight, only a person such as I who looks at it every day would notice the shift.'

'How can a rock as old as time change its position, except during an earthquake?' Professor Scott asked.

'There have been no earth tremors,' the boy replied. 'The rock has moved for some other reason.'

'We must go over there and investigate!' Susan Sand exclaimed. 'There is some sensible explanation. Who better than Black Cloud and Brave Deer to show us the way?'

18

Journey up the mountain

'We will take you to Fawn Rock,' said Black Cloud.
'There is a path up the mountain, but it is not easy to find.
Come. We must go along the creek to the footbridge and
take the trail through the woods. It is not so direct, but it is
the easiest way.'

'We could set out from here and go across the valley,'
explained Brave Deer, 'but the route is very rugged. My
uncle is right. We must go to the bridge. Whenever people
from the inn make the journey, they always take the path
from the creek.'

'Then lead the way,' said Susan Sand. 'We'll be right
behind you.'

'I feel like a pioneer,' squealed Marge. 'How long will it
take?'

'An hour, perhaps,' said Black Cloud, shrugging his
massive shoulders.

The group set out from the cavern and walked single file
along the Feather Creek to the footbridge, where they
turned into the woods. Black Cloud led the way, with
Brave Deer and Wolf Dog close behind. The path through
the forest was barely perceptible to the four friends, but
the Indians had no trouble in following it and trudged
along in silence, maintaining a steady pace and never
turning around. The way went gradually up, and
although the day was hot, the air in the woods was cool
and damp.

Within half an hour they had reached a point where the

ground levelled off and became more rocky. The trees began to thin out, and the air became warmer. Black Cloud led them sharply to the right and spoke for the first time since their departure from the cavern.

'You will have to be much more careful from now on,' he warned them. 'The path from here to Fawn Rock is treacherous, and you must watch your footing.'

The group followed the Indian's advice and began to tread much more slowly over the rocky ground.

'I'm beginning to feel tired,' whispered Marge to Brian, who was directly behind her.

'Perhaps you would like me to carry you,' he replied.

Marge looked up at him and made a face.

'Why don't we ask Black Cloud to stop and rest?' suggested Susan, who was in front of Marge and heard her comment.

'Is something wrong?' the older Indian asked, stopping and turning around.

'Marge is tired,' said Susan before the redhead had a chance to stop her.

'Then we will all sit down,' Black Cloud commanded. 'There is a stream near here. I will get some water.'

He pulled a flask from under his buckskin jacket and set off into the woods. In five minutes he returned and offered the flask to Marge, who gratefully drank the cold, sparkling water. The container was handed around, and the group rested for another ten minutes before setting out again.

As they continued their journey Brave Deer, who was just in front of Susan, turned around and spoke to her.

'Someone has been along here recently,' he said, his voice low. 'I noticed it ever since we started from the footbridge. My uncle and I used to take parties to Fawn Rock, but we have not done so for several years because people complained and did not seem to enjoy themselves.'

'Who would take such a trip, and without you and your uncle as guides?' asked Susan.

'It is interesting,' Brave Deer responded. 'I am anxious to reach Fawn Rock and investigate.'

'So am I, Brave Deer,' Susan agreed.

Randall Scott, who had been in the rear of the party, caught up with Susan and took her arm. 'What are you whispering about?' he asked.

'Brave Deer says that someone has been along this path recently,' she replied.

'Really!' the young man exclaimed, raising his eyebrows. 'No one would take this track except to reach Fawn Rock.'

'Exactly,' Susan said.

They fell into silence again, and Randall Scott returned to his place at the end of the line. Within ten minutes Black Cloud held up his hand, and everyone stopped.

'There is Fawn Rock,' he announced, pointing towards a long, massive stone that jutted out from the side of the mountain.

Wolf Dog, who had been quiet and well behaved during the trip, started to bark excitedly and ran out onto the rock.

'Oh, Brave Deer!' cried Marge. 'Aren't you afraid she will fall?'

'No, she has done that many times,' he replied. 'She will not go too near the edge.'

'It is a tremendous drop,' commented Professor Scott. 'What a view this is, with the falls over there across the valley. We are certainly very high up.'

Black Cloud walked to the rock, his eyes on the ground. 'Someone has been here,' he said, bending down next to a patch of soft earth.

'You found a footprint!' cried Susan, rushing to the Indian's side. 'It is very clear.'

'Yes, a woman's foot, or a small man's,' he replied, outlining the print with his finger. 'It was made yesterday or today, since the rain stopped.'

'Look at this,' called Brave Deer, who had crawled down an incline alongside Fawn Rock. 'The ground underneath the rock has been disturbed. Someone has been digging.'

'Digging!' exclaimed Susan, leaning over the edge of the slope and peering at the spot the boy indicated.

'Yes. Here is a pile of dirt.'

Carefully Susan Sand made her way down the slope and joined Brave Deer, who was looking into an enormous hole that had been excavated beneath Fawn Rock.

'The entire rock has sunk because of this hole,' he said to Susan. 'The rain has softened the earth even more. That is why I noticed the change in the rock when I looked through the falls.'

Black Cloud, Randall Scott, Marge, and Brian gathered on the edge of the cliff and stood looking down at Susan and Brave Deer.

'Who would come here and dig under Fawn Rock?' Brian asked. 'And why?'

'I opt for the "Tanners",' replied Marge. 'That footprint could fit either of them.'

'I think you are right, Marge,' Susan answered. 'But what were they looking for? Why would two middle-aged people make such a difficult journey up the mountain?'

'And when they got here, they had to dig,' added Brian. 'I call that motivation.'

Susan Sand sat back on her heels and bit her lip, her green eyes looking far off across the valley.

'I doubt that they would bring the tools with them each time,' she reasoned. 'They must be hidden somewhere around here.'

'They should not be hard to find,' said Black Cloud, retreating into the forest that surrounded Fawn Rock and scanning the ground. 'Here is another footprint, and it leads directly into the woods.'

He made his way through the trees and disappeared

from view, only to return a short time later carrying a pick-axe and two shovels.

'These were hidden very inexpertly among some shrubbery,' he told them.

'Obviously whoever did this digging didn't expect to be found out,' Susan commented. 'Now I see why you were frightened away from the falls, Brave Deer. The "Tanners", if they are the culprits, were concerned that you would notice the change in Fawn Rock, so they thought up the scheme using Claudia to keep you from the falls.'

'She must be extremely afraid of them,' the boy replied, his brow knitted. 'They are dangerous people. How I wish she had come to me and told me everything!'

'She has been protecting you, Brave Deer,' said Susan gently. 'She must have thought that the safest thing to do was to obey them.'

'Brave Deer has told me about the wax,' said Black Cloud angrily.

'Finding the wax is an important step,' replied Susan. 'But we need more evidence before the "Tanners" can be accused of the robberies. I would like to know what Barry Hearne has to do with this.'

'Perhaps Mr Kingsley is also involved,' offered Brave Deer. 'Claudia is afraid of her father. He makes her work too hard. He knows that I do not like it.'

'There is nothing more we can do here,' said Susan, getting to her feet and brushing herself off. 'Let's get back to the inn. Tonight Randall and I are going to the Smythe Farmhouse to investigate the storage room.'

'Why do you want to do that?' Black Cloud asked.

'I found a used flashbulb in the room where the shutters are stored,' explained Susan.

'A used flashbulb!' he exclaimed.

'Both the "Tanners" and Barry Hearne stayed in the farmhouse,' said Randall Scott. 'Someone went into the storage room and took pictures.'

116

'How extraordinary!' said Black Cloud, more animated than Susan had ever seen him. 'Mrs "Tanner" always has a camera. Perhaps she is the one who was taking pictures.'

'I don't see what connection that can have with this digging under Fawn Rock,' said Marge.

'There may not be any relation,' said Susan Sand. 'But the pieces will all fit together eventually. Let's get back to the inn. I can hadly wait until tonight.'

19

In the storage room

Black Cloud returned the tools to their hiding place, and the group set off down the mountain. The sun was beginning to set, and a refreshing coolness brushed their faces. When they reached the footbridge, Brave Deer and Black Cloud bade them farewell and headed for the older Indian's cabin.

'They are concerned that I will get into trouble tonight,' said Susan, smiling. 'Brave Deer feels that it is his responsibility to investigate the storeroom himself.'

'He is extremely worried about Claudia also,' offered Marge. 'He is very protective towards her.'

At the inn, Susan went to Mrs Vandervelden's room to talk to her about the robberies, but a hotel maid said that she had returned to New York City for a few days.

'Mrs Vandervelden is on all sorts of committees,' said Susan when she entered her room, where Marge, Brian, and Randall were talking about the plans for that night. 'I am certain she will be back for the next camping trip.'

Late that night, Susan Sand and Randall Scott, dressed in dark clothing, started for the Smythe farmhouse. Susan had learned from Brave Deer that no one was staying in the room where Brian and the professor had slept the night before. As they neared the dark structure, Susan felt a thrill of excitement, for she sensed that she was on the verge of an important discovery.

The pair soon found a ladder, which had been left by

some workmen lying alongside the back of the house. Together they carried it beneath the storage-room window and placed it carefully against the wall.

'You stay below and hold the ladder for me,' whispered Susan. 'That window is so small, it's more sensible for me to try to get into the room. Besides, I need a lookout.'

'What do I do if someone should come along?' asked Randall Scott, his brown eyes twinkling.

'Perhaps you could say you are having a rendezvous with your secret lover,' rejoined Susan, starting up the ladder.

'Who happens to be a detective and insists on taking all sorts of chances,' he joked, his voice low.

At the top of the ladder Susan steadied herself and attempted to open the window. At first it resisted her efforts, but eventually she managed to push it up far enough to climb through into the room. Once inside, Susan took the torch from her pocket and switched it on.

'This floor looks safe enough to me,' she thought, stepping carefully to the centre of the room.

For several moments Susan studied the little room and tried the door, which was still locked. Then she found the flashbulb lying in the crack between the floorboards and placed it in her pocket.

'Why was Mrs "Tanner" taking pictures?' she mused. 'And of what? If the person was Mrs "Tanner". These shutters seem to be the only things in this room, and they look as if they have been here for many years.'

Susan studied the floor and could see definite indications of footprints, for the dust was disturbed, especially at one end of the room.

'These shutters must have been the centre of interest,' Susan decided. 'How odd! Oh, no, here is a pile of newspapers.'

Jubilantly Susan knelt down and pulled the yellowed papers towards her.

'Is it possible that there is something in one of these

papers that could shed light on this mystery?' she wondered. 'They are dated many years ago.'

Rising, Susan went to the window and called softly to Randall Scott, who was still holding the ladder. 'Randall, I found a pile of newspapers. It will take some time for me to go through them.'

'Perhaps we should take them with us,' he suggested.

'No, I don't think that would be wise,' Susan answered. 'Their loss might be discovered. I will just have to stay here until I have gone through all of them.'

'Then let me come up and help you,' he insisted, starting up the ladder.

'No, Randall. It would be much safer if you put the ladder back where we found it. Then, when I am finished, I will call to you and you can replace it so I can get down. In that way no one will know we are here.'

'As much as I dislike the idea, I think you are right,' he replied, lifting the ladder away from the house. 'I'll put the ladder back and hide myself in the shrubbery. A nice occupation for a distinguished college professor!'

Susan returned to the pile of newspapers and sat down on the dirty floor. Balancing her torch in her lap, she began the arduous task of going through every page. Slowly she turned the pages and scanned each item. Half an hour later she had managed to look through only a small portion of the pile.

'This will take me a good part of the night,' she moaned, rising and stretching herself. 'And I don't even know what I am looking for.'

Returning to the window, Susan leaned out and called softly to Randall, but he did not answer.

'Randall,' she called again, more loudly, but the young man did not appear.

'Where could he be?' she asked herself. 'Perhaps he just got tired and felt like some exercise,' she decided, but her mind was uneasy.

'There is nothing for me to do but continue my reading,'

she thought and sat down again on the floor. Her mind wandered, however, for it was not like Randall Scott to desert her on such a risky mission. Twice she went back to the window, but he did not respond when she called to him.

'Now I really am beginning to get worried,' she thought. 'Where could he be? And me trapped up here with the door locked!'

Tired and worried, Susan thrust the newspaper she was reading aside and sat back on her heels. Her eyes travelled to the window shutters that were lined up neatly against the wall, and she suddenly noticed something that had escaped her before.

'That shutter has been dusted off,' she said to herself, getting to her feet and lifting the heavy shutter away from the wall.

Susan studied the front of the shutter and then turned it around. 'Why, there's writing on the back!' she thought in amazement. 'It is very faint, but it is readable.'

Her blood rushing in her veins, Susan carefully leaned the shutter against the wall and bent down to study the writing.

'Oh, I can barely make it out,' she thought anxiously, adjusting her glasses and narrowing her eyes. 'This old handwriting is hard to decipher because the letters are formed differently.'

Realising she had made a significant find, Susan Sand tried to suppress her excitement. Slowly she traced the faint words with her finger, not touching the shutter for fear of obliterating them.

'It seems to say:

"White Rabbit outwitted Dayonas. Hid Pipe in Fawn Rock. Came here."

And it's signed W.S. – William Smythe! What a discovery! The hiding place of the Pipe of Peace is in Fawn Rock. This writing has been on the shutter for well over three hundred years, but apparently no one found it until now. Mrs "Tanner" must have photographed this message in order to study it.'

Nearly trembling with excitement, Susan Sand rushed to the window and called Randall Scott's name, but still he did not respond.

'What has happened to him?' she said out loud. 'I've made this incredible discovery, and now I can't get down to the ground to look for him! What am I to do?'

Restlessly, Susan returned to the window shutter and memorised the message. 'No wonder the "Tanners" were digging under Fawn Rock,' she thought. 'How I wish I knew if they have found the Pipe of Peace!'

Forcing herself to remain calm, Susan repeated the message over and over until she was certain she had learned it by heart, for she had nothing on which to write it down.

'This proves that White Rabbit was trying to prevent the Pipe of Peace from falling into the hands of the Dayonas,' Susan reasoned. 'He had the pipe on his back in a leather bag, according to Rose Petal, and was supposed to run to the cavern behind the falls, where the seven chiefs were meeting. He feared the Dayonas would attack him, so he hid the pipe in Fawn Rock, ran to this farm-house, and told Farmer Smythe where the pipe was. The Dayonas followed him, for the farmer was found dead the next day downstairs. But before he died, he managed to write this message on the back of the shutter.'

Susan switched off the torch and went back to the window. Randall Scott was not there.

'I must escape from this room and find out what has happened to him,' Susan decided.

Crossing quietly to the door, she studied the lock. 'I have picked locks in the past,' she mused, 'but this one poses problems.'

Suddenly Susan heard a noise in the bedroom beyond. Someone had closed the door to the hall and was walking across the room. Several seconds later the handle of the storage room turned.

Remaining completely motionless, Susan Sand drew in her breath and waited. The person on the other side pushed heavily against the door and continued to turn the knob. After several tries, they gave up, and soon the other room was silent.

'What a close shave!' thought Susan. 'If the person had been Randall, he would have identified himself. Besides, he would never enter the house, knowing I would be waiting for him to replacc the ladder.'

Susan's relief was short-lived, however, for within five minutes there was noise outside the tiny window of the storage room. Expecting to see Randall Scott waiting below, Susan rushed to the window and looked out. Barry Hearne had placed the ladder against the house and was climbing quickly towards her!

20

Plans

'Barry Hearne!' cried Susan Sand, completely stunned.

'Susan, listen,' he called up to her. 'There is something—'

Before he could utter another word, Randall Scott came running from around the side of the house and, with a flying tackle, threw himself on Barry Hearne. He grasped the man's legs, pulled him from the ladder, and wrestled him to the ground. The ladder rocked precariously back and forth, but Susan managed to steady it and then quickly climbed down.

'Please listen to me,' gasped Barry Hearne, desperately trying to defend himself against Randall Scott's fists. 'I am not a thief. I am a detective hired by Mrs Vandervelden.'

'A detective!' exclaimed Susan, grabbing Randall Scott by the shoulders and attempting to calm him down. 'Please, Randall, let him speak.'

'Don't trust him, Sue,' the young man retorted, his hair in wild disarray and one eye bruised and swollen. 'He surprised me before when I was putting the ladder back and knocked me out without any explanation. He never would have managed it if he hadn't jumped me from behind.'

'I didn't know who you were,' Barry Hearne began, freeing himself from the professor's grasp. 'Please accept my apologies. We should be working together on this. If you will just let me explain . . .'

'You better make it good,' Randall Scott said, pulling Susan to his side.

'Mrs Vandvervelden hired me last spring, right after her apartment was robbed,' the man began. 'She suspected that in some way the robberies were connected with the Feather Inn, but she had no way of finding out the truth herself.'

'Why didn't you tell us this before?' Randall Scott asked, running his fingers through his rumpled hair. 'It seems to me all you've been doing is following Susan around.'

'I didn't want to take anyone into my confidence,' replied Barry Hearne, adjusting his torn jacket. 'I realise now that I was wrong, but I promised Mrs Vandervelden that I would say nothing to anyone.'

'How is it that Mrs Vandervelden knows you?' asked Susan.

'I used to be on the New York City police force,' the man answered. 'I knew Mrs V. very well because she is so active in civic affairs and I was on a committee with her. Naturally, when these robberies occurred, she immediately thought of me because I had left the force to start my own detective agency.'

Barry Hearne reached into his trousers pocket and pulled out a wallet. Opening it, he handed it to Susan. 'This is my identification,' he stated. 'I am a licensed private detective. When we get back to the inn, I'll call Mrs V. herself, and you can ask her.'

'Then you are not interested in writing at all,' replied Susan, starting to laugh. 'You joined my seminar as a cover.'

'That's right, Susan,' Barry Hearne rejoined, grinning. 'I never had any talent in writing, nor any interest, either. Joining the seminar was Mrs V.'s idea. She paid for the whole thing. She felt that someone might get on to me because I look so much like a policeman.'

'You sure have a powerful right,' retorted Randall Scott, rubbing his jaw.

'And you do look like a policeman,' added Susan. 'I should have realised that the minute I saw you.'

'There is one thing that I have learned from all of this,' said Barry Hearne. 'You are a better detective than I am, Miss Susan Sand. If I had been wise, I would have joined up with you right away instead of tailing you all over the place, even up to that storage room.'

'Thank you for the compliment,' Susan replied.

'And accept my apologies,' offered Randall Scott, shaking Barry Hearne's hand. 'You've been on our list of suspects for some time.'

'The sensible thing for us to do is pool our knowledge,' suggested Susan. 'We must catch the "Tanners" at their robberies and find out if they have unearthed the Pipe of Peace.'

Quickly Susan told the two men of her discovery on the window shutter. They listened, fascinated, while she related the message that Farmer Smythe had written so many centuries ago.

'That's an incredible bit of detective work, Susan,' said Barry Hearne. 'But I can tell you that the "Tanners" did not find the pipe. Yesterday I followed them to the site at Fawn Rock. I couldn't imagine why they were digging there, but I heard enough to know what they were looking for and that they didn't find it. They were very angry and tired after all that shovelling.'

'We were at Fawn Rock today,' said Susan. 'Black Cloud and Brave Deer took us. We didn't find any of your footprints.'

'I am not that bad a detective,' the young man replied, laughing heartily. 'Any footprints I made up there I removed.'

'So the "Tanners" not only have been committing the robberies, but they have also been looking for the Pipe of Peace,' commented Professor Scott. 'They've had their fingers in each pie.'

'When they stayed here at the farmhouse, the door to

126

the storage room was unlocked,' said Susan. 'They discovered that message and photographed it in order to study it. But since they haven't found the pipe, where could it be?'

'That's a mystery I haven't solved,' Barry Hearne replied. 'Mrs V. hired me to get the goods on them over these robberies, and I got side-tracked. Now I find that I am involved with a peace pipe over three hundred years old.'

'We must catch the "Tanners" at their regular game,' retorted Susan, 'the robberies.'

Quickly she told Barry Hearne about her discovery of the wax in the 'Tanners'' bathroom.

'That's evidence, Susan!' exclaimed Barry Hearne. 'But not enough to get them behind bars. Now we know how your cat got the wax on his paw.'

'He must have been in their room when they were taking impressions of the keys,' Susan returned, 'and they didn't know he was there.'

'Let's get back to the inn,' interjected Randall Scott. 'Marge and Brian will call out the police if we don't show up soon!'

'And we can lay our plans for catching these crooks,' said Barry Hearne heatedly.

After returning the ladder, Randall Scott and Susan accompanied their new friend back to the Feather Inn and hurried to Susan's room, where Marge and Brian awaited them.

'A detective!' cried Marge, her eyes wide with amazement. 'We thought you were a crook.'

'It's a good thing Professor Scott found out your identity before he killed you, Mr Hearne,' added Brian with a laugh.

'It was touch and go there for a while,' Barry Hearne joked, indicating his torn jacket and bruised face.

'It seems to me that Mrs Vandervelden could have been more honest with you, Sue,' said Randall Scott in his most dignified manner. 'None of this would have happened if you had known who Mr Hearne was.'

'I can understand Mrs Vandervelden's position,' Susan answered. 'She was only doing what she thought best.'

Barry Hearne glanced at his watch. 'Two-twenty in the morning!' he exclaimed. 'I can't call Mrs V. at this hour, but as soon as the sun is up, I'll give her a ring and tell her what has happened.'

'Let's all get some sleep,' suggested Susan. 'Remember, the "Tanners" don't suspect us, so we must not be seen together as if we are conspiring. I will still act as though I don't know you well, Mr Hearne. Tomorrow we can lay our plans for their capture.'

Everyone slept late, and Susan and Marge did not go down to breakfast until after ten o'clock. Randall Scott and Brian were already eating, and the girls joined them at their table.

'Randall, your face looks terrible,' whispered Susan.

'Wait until you see Barry Hearne's,' rejoined Brian. 'He just finished his breakfast.'

'If the "Tanners" see both of you, they will know that you two had a fight,' replied Susan.

'That's better than having them think we are friends,' reasoned the professor.

Just then Mrs Vandervelden entered the dining-room and seated herself at a nearby table. Smiling, she waved to the four friends but made no attempt to speak to them, for at that moment the 'Tanners' came in, sat down not far away, and said good morning to everyone.

'Barry Hearne must have called Mrs Vandervelden,' said Marge quietly, acknowledging the new arrivals.

'The "Tanners" appear to be all ready for another day among the wild flowers,' commented Brian dryly. 'Mrs "Tanner" has her camera, and he is carrying that black box he uses for his flower collection.'

'What frauds they are!' murmured Susan under her

128

breath. 'Just wait until we catch them. They won't look so smug.'

'Look, there's Claudia!' exclaimed Marge. 'How pale she is!'

Mrs Vandervelden signalled to the girl, and Claudia immediately went to her table to pour her coffee. The older woman spoke to her for several moments, and then Claudia came over to the four friends and greeted them cheerfully.

As she bent over the table to fill Susan's cup, she whispered in her ear, 'Come to Black Cloud's cabin in an hour.'

Still smiling, Claudia finished filling the cups, took their orders, and returned to the kitchen. Susan, her face not betraying the excitement she felt, looked at her three friends.

'The plans are being laid in Black Cloud's cabin,' she said in a low voice, the coffee cup at her lips. 'Barry Hearne has been busy this morning. I think we are closing in on the "Tanners"!'

21

Susan is not satisfied

An hour later, Susan went to Black Cloud's cabin alone. Randall Scott, Brian, and Marge had agreed that if the 'Tanners' were at all suspicious, they might be watching to see what the four friends would do. Susan on her own could reach the cabin with less chance of being observed. When she knocked on the door and was admitted by Brave Deer, Mrs Vandervelden and Claudia were seated in the living-room.

'Susan!' exclaimed the older woman, jumping to her feet and taking Susan's hand. 'I am truly sorry that Barry and I caused you so much trouble. I was foolish not to take you into my confidence, but we both thought we should keep his identity a secret.'

'I understand, Mrs Vandervelden,' Susan replied graciously. 'But we did have Mr Hearne as a prime suspect.'

'The "Tanners" have been the guilty ones,' said Black Cloud, emerging from another room and greeting Susan. 'Mrs Vandervelden has told Brave Deer and me what you discovered in the Smythe farmhouse.'

'Barry informed me of your find, Susan,' said Mrs Vandervelden. 'To think that the "Tanners" not only have been robbing guests, but also are trying to make off with a valuable piece of history!'

'So much of this could have been prevented if I had been honest,' Claudia burst out, her eyes filling with tears. 'Oh, why didn't I tell you the truth?'

'I have been attempting to convince Claudia that she did no wrong,' said Mrs Vandervelden kindly. 'She has been terrified by the "Tanners". They threatened to harm her father and Brave Deer if she said anything to anybody.'

'I didn't know what to do,' the girl cried, wringing her hands. 'Miss Sand, I am so sorry. Mrs Tanner hit Marge Halloran over the head, and then they trapped you in the tunnel, and it's all my fault!' The blonde girl burst into tears and threw herself into Mrs Vandervelden's lap.

'Poor child,' said the woman, stroking Claudia's hair. 'She was even afraid to tell her own father.'

'Has Mr Kingsley been told yet?' Susan asked.

'Yes. I spoke to him earlier,' Mrs Vandervelden replied. 'He has been so concerned with running the inn, it never occurred to him that his own daughter was in danger, in the clutches of criminals. He wanted to rush off to the police, but I convinced him that we must get real evidence. Barry and I have been talking, and we have come up with a plan. Right now he is in New York, talking to the police.'

'Come, Claudia,' said Brave Deer, taking the girl's hand and pulling her to her feet. 'We will go for a walk in the woods. I do not want you to be involved any longer in this. You must come with me, and we will take our favourite trail.'

'But – but I want to hear what you are planning,' Claudia stammered. 'After all, I did play the "Phantom", so I feel that I should help to catch the "Tanners". Isn't there anything I can do?'

'No, dear,' Mrs Vandervelden replied. 'You go with Brave Deer and try to forget all about this. The "Tanners" will never hurt you again.'

'Mrs Vandervelden is right, Claudia,' said Susan. 'Leave the "Tanners" to us.'

'Thank goodness that is settled!' exclaimed Mrs Vandervelden when Claudia and Brave Deer, followed by

Wolf Dog, had left the cabin. 'That poor child needs to have some fun.'

'I considered her father as a suspect,' Susan revealed, sitting down. 'Especially when he locked the door to the storage room and said he thought the floor might be unsafe. Now I realise he was sincere and had nothing to do with the "Tanners" at all.'

'Warren Kingsley has been blind, Susan,' retorted Mrs Vandervelden angrily. 'He has not paid enough attention to Claudia, but I am certain things will be different in the future.'

'Brave Deer is entirely capable of caring for Claudia,' Susan answered. 'Now tell me, Mrs Vandervelden, what you and Barry Hearne have planned.'

'I own an extremely valuable emerald necklace,' began Mrs Vandervelden. 'I will tell the "Tanners" how relieved I was that the necklace was in my safe deposit box when my apartment was robbed. Then, casually, as if I have no suspicions of them whatsoever, I will let them know that the necklace is now in my jewellery case in my apartment.'

'And I am going to announce a camping trip, which is to start tomorrow morning,' Black Cloud revealed. 'This will give the "Tanners" an opportunity to rob the apartment again.'

'What a clever plan!' Susan replied. 'How I would like to be there and see them caught!'

'Barry will take care of that,' the older woman said. 'Why don't you and your friends come on the camping trip with us? You don't know what fun it is, sleeping outside and cooking over an open fire. It's exciting and challenging.'

'I would like to come,' Susan decided. 'And my friends will, too. But we don't have sleeping-bags, except for Brian Lorenzo, or any other equipment that we might need.'

'Everything necessary for the trip can be rented at the

132

inn,' Black Cloud told her. 'You must wear good soft shoes, sensible clothing, and follow my orders.'

'Just as if we were in the army,' said Mrs Vandervelden, laughing. 'Black Cloud is a first-rate sergeant.'

'I am looking forward to the trip already!' Susan exclaimed. 'But I could enjoy it even more if I knew where the Pipe of Peace is. Since Barry Hearne is certain that the "Tanners" haven't found it, where can it be?'

'It is possible that the pipe was found many years ago,' Black Cloud stated.

'You may be right, Black Cloud,' Susan replied, rising to her feet. 'But it is very frustrating not to know what happened to it.'

'You go back to the inn and prepare for the camping trip, Susan,' Mrs Vandervelden advised.

'We leave promptly at eight o'clock in the morning,' Black Cloud informed her. 'We will all meet in front of the inn.'

'May I bring my cat?' Susan asked. 'He loves the woods, and I haven't had much time to spend with him. He would very much enjoy a camping trip.'

'Of course you may bring him,' replied Black Cloud, smiling. 'Since he and Wolf Dog get along so well, they will take pleasure in each other's company.'

'Then it's all settled,' said Susan, turning to the door. 'If everything goes as planned, the "Tanners" will soon be behind bars.'

She bade goodbye to Mrs Vandervelden and Black Cloud and started back through the woods.

'Why does the message say "in" Fawn Rock?' she wondered. 'Nothing can be hidden "in" a rock, yet that is definitely what Farmer Smythe wrote.'

Turning the matter over in her mind, Susan Sand walked slowly through the forest until she emerged at Feather Creek, where she continued along the path. A short distance from the inn an idea occurred to her.

'When we were at the museum, Rose Petal showed us a

map,' Susan recalled. 'It was an old map of this area on display in one of the showcases. Perhaps I will see something on it that I overlooked before.'

When Susan reached the inn she went directly to her car and drove off to the town of Featherford. Fortunately, the museum was open and Rose Petal came forward to greet her.

'Miss Sand, how nice to see you again,' the Indian woman said pleasantly.

'Rose Petal, one reason I have come is to return this to you,' Susan replied, pulling a white envelope from her purse. 'I found this feather near the falls.'

'This is the same black feather that was stolen!' Rose Petal exclaimed, opening the envelope. 'Oh, how glad I am to get it back! Thank you, Susan. You say you found it near the falls?'

'Yes, but I can't explain the circumstances just yet. In a short time I will be able to tell you everything. Can you accept that explanation for the time being?'

'Of course, Susan,' the woman answered. 'I am so happy to have it back. I will lock it up so no one can take it again.'

'I would like to have another look at that old parchment map,' Susan said, crossing to the showcase.

Leaning over the glass top, she began to study the details of the old chart. Fortunately, Rose Petal had a magnifying-glass, and Susan was able to make out many words which otherwise would have been illegible. So intent was she on her task, she was not aware that another person had entered the museum.

'That's an interesting map, isn't it, Miss Sand?' said a voice over her shoulder.

'Yes, it is,' replied Susan, turning around. 'Why, Mr Tanner! I didn't expect to see you here.'

22

Susan's victory

'I thought you would be out with your wife,' said Susan, turning back to the map. 'This is a lovely day for collecting wild flowers.'

'Oh, we have a splendid trip planned,' Mr 'Tanner' replied pleasantly. 'This entire area is full of the most wonderful specimens.'

'I am very excited about tomorrow, because Black Cloud is taking Mrs Vandervelden and my friends and me on a camping trip,' Susan told him. 'I hope the weather is as fine as today. We expect to be gone until Sunday.'

'Black Cloud is a most unusual person,' Mr 'Tanner' answered, studying the map alongside Susan. 'Just where is he taking you? North, towards Fawn Rock, or south? The woods are thick all around this area.'

'I really don't know, Mr Tanner,' Susan truthfully replied. 'We will leave that up to Black Cloud. Have you found what you were looking for on this map?'

'Yes, I believe I have,' he said. 'I just wanted to check on a spot up past the falls. Sometimes old maps are more informative than recent ones.'

Mr 'Tanner' said goodbye to Susan and left the museum, after wishing her a successful camping expedition.

'Was his coming here coincidence, or did he follow me?' Susan asked herself.

For ten more minutes Susan studied the map. Then she thanked Rose Petal, left the museum, and returned to the inn. Upon reaching her room, she called Randall and

135

Brian, and soon all four friends were talking about Susan's trip to Black Cloud's cabin. Briefly, she outlined the plan to catch the 'Tanners' and she told them about her meeting with Mr 'Tanner' at the museum.

'I'll bet he tailed you there,' said Professor Scott. 'He must suspect something.'

'At least I had a good chance to tell him about the camping trip,' Susan replied. 'Mrs Vandervelden will casually inform Mrs "Tanner" about her emerald necklace, and if they fall for the bait, one or both of them will go to New York within the next few days to steal it.'

'While we are off in the woods having a great time!' exclaimed Marge.

'What did you find on that old map?' Brian asked.

'I am not certain if I discovered anything,' Susan replied. 'But I tried to memorise as much of it as I could. There are quite a few spots that no longer appear on the new maps. Somehow I feel that there is something I have overlooked.'

'You can think about it while we are on the trip,' responded Marge. 'Let's go and pack.'

By the following morning, all was in order for the expedition into the woods. Food for the journey had been prepared by Claudia, who was outside the inn early to bid them goodbye. Mysteriously, Susan was missing, but just as the group was about to depart she rushed around the corner of the hotel.

'I went back to the museum, and Rose Petal found me a copy of that old map,' she explained breathlessly, displaying a rolled-up piece of paper. 'Fortunately she was there. She lives upstairs.'

'Then let's get under way,' said Mrs Vandervelden cheerfully.

'Icky is very excited,' commented Marge, who was holding the marmalade animal in her arms. 'He knows we are going on an adventure.'

'Come, Wolf Dog,' said Brave Deer.

'In which direction are we heading, Black Cloud?' asked Professor Scott.

'I will take us north over the Feather Creek,' the Indian informed them. 'We will walk at a slow pace so no one will get too tired.'

Their sleeping-bags on their backs, the party started off amid shouts and waves from other guests who were not making the trip. Wolf Dog ran ahead, barking, for she knew the route Black Cloud intended to take.

'It is Wolf Dog's favourite trail,' said Brave Deer. 'She knows where we are going.'

'Isn't this great fun, Susan?' said Mrs Vandervelden, walking alongside her. Then, lowering her voice, she whispered in Susan's ear, 'I told Mrs "Tanner" about the necklace, and her eyes lit up like a Christmas tree. I would bet my entire fortune that she will try to steal that necklace today.'

'Oh, I hope you are right,' Susan rejoined.

By noon the group had penetrated far into the woods. Removing their back packs, they all sat on the ground to enjoy lunch. Leaning against a tree, Susan spread out the map in her lap and began to study it.

'Sue, can't you forget about that map?' Randall Scott chided.

'No, Randall, I intend to find that Pipe of Peace,' Susan said determinedly.

'Susan can't help being a detective,' chimed in Marge. 'Holidays mean nothing to her. Always work, work, work!'

'Stop teasing her,' said Brian in a mischievous tone. 'Sue likes to detect, and you like to eat.'

The four friends had chosen a spot somewhat removed from the rest of the party. Mrs Vandervelden was chatting amiably with several other campers, and there was no one nearby when Susan made her discovery.

'Look at this,' she said, pointing to a spot on the map. 'Doesn't that say "Far Oak"?'

'Yes, I can see it does,' said Professor Scott.

'Then that's it!' cried Susan, her eyes gleaming.

'That's what?' asked Marge.

'I've been reading the message wrong,' Susan replied. 'I made the same mistake the "Tanners" did. Farmer Smythe didn't write "Fawn Rock". He wrote "Far Oak". The Pipe of Peace is hidden in Far Oak. That must be the answer! There is no other spot on this map that remotely resembles the words "Fawn Rock".'

'Sue, I think you are absolutely right!' exclaimed Randall Scott.

The four friends decided that Farmer Smythe's old-fashioned handwriting, blurred by time, was the reason the message was read incorrectly.

'The letters written on the shutter are run together,' Susan explained. 'Since I'd never heard of Far Oak, it was only natural to read the words as "Fawn Rock".'

'But Sue, how can you find a tree in a forest of trees?' asked Marge.

'I will ask Black Cloud if he has ever heard of Far Oak,' replied Susan.

Susan went and brought the older Indian over to their picnic site. Showing him the map, she pointed to the words 'Far Oak'.

'Yes, I have heard of Far Oak,' Black Cloud said. 'It was once a magnificent tree, hundreds of years old, but it was hit by lightning and is no longer there.'

'Oh, dear,' moaned Marge. 'Well, it was a good idea, Sue.'

'Just because the tree is gone doesn't mean that the pipe isn't there,' Susan insisted. 'If White Rabbit hid the pipe in the hollow of the oak, it may be there still. If only we can find the stump of the tree!'

'I can find Far Oak,' Black Cloud stated. 'My people recorded certain trail points, and Far Oak was one of them. But I can't leave the camping party.'

'Then you must tell me how to get there, Black Cloud,'

Susan told him. 'We must reach Far Oak before the "Tanners" make the same discovery.'

'You would never be able to find it,' Black Cloud said. 'Only someone with a complete knowledge of these woods could follow the trail.'

'Black Cloud, I must get to Far Oak!' Susan pleaded.

'Yes, we must see if it is possible that the Pipe of Peace is really there after all this time,' Black Cloud agreed. 'But do not worry that the "Tanners" will get there first, Susan.'

'Since you can't leave the camping party, what can we do?' asked Brian.

'I will take us along another trail,' Black Cloud decided. 'By nightfall we will be very close to Far Oak. When the sun comes up tomorrow morning, I will take you to the spot.'

'Oh, Black Cloud, thank you!' cried Susan. 'Think of what it will mean for your people to have the Pipe of Peace returned to them!'

'It will mean a great deal,' the Indian said quietly. 'It will prove that White Rabbit was not a coward.'

By nightfall, the group was exhausted and climbed wearily into their sleeping-bags. Icky and Wolf Dog curled up side by side near the campfire, while Brave Deer, sitting on his haunches, stirred the dying embers.

Before dawn, Susan rose and shook Randall Scott. Black Cloud had already started a fire and was making breakfast.

'Randall, let's not wake Marge and Brian,' she whispered. 'Black Cloud can take us to find the pipe, and we will be back before the sun is up.'

Professor Scott grunted some unintelligible words and went back to sleep. Smiling, Susan went to the campfire and said good morning to their guide.

'Professor Scott prefers to sleep,' she said.

'He is not as adventurous as you,' replied Black Cloud,

handing Susan a cup of steaming coffee. 'Eat your breakfast, and we will go to Far Oak.'

Silently, Susan ate a bowl of cornflakes.

'We have been followed,' Black Cloud informed her, an amused expression on his face.

'Followed!' Susan said softly.

'Yes. Mr "Tanner" thinks he is being clever. He is hiding in the woods. We will let him trail us to Far Oak.'

'I might have known that he realised he had made a mistake in digging under Fawn Rock,' replied Susan. 'That's why he followed me into the museum. He is going to let us find the pipe and then attempt to steal it.'

'He will not get the pipe if we are successful in finding it,' said Black Cloud.

Together Susan and Black Cloud started for Far Oak and were joined by Brave Deer and Wolf Dog. They did not speak as they walked swiftly along the trail. Never had Susan Sand experienced such a thrill of anticipation. Treading quickly through the forest between the two Indians, she felt as though the entire world was remote and that nothing mattered but the journey. Every so often she thought she heard a rustling behind them, but she saw nothing.

'There is the spot,' Black Cloud announced a short time later. 'Yes, that is the stump of Far Oak. See, there is a great deal of debris from the storm that caused the tree to fall.'

The three approached the site and started to clear away the leaves, fallen branches, and shrubs that covered the huge stump. The task took some time, but eventually they had uncovered the stump to discover a gaping hole. Brave Deer reached down into the hollow and groped expectantly.

'There is something here,' he said, his torso resting on the edge of the stump and his body nearly perpendicular. 'It is a box!'

Susan and Black Cloud held on to the boy while he

struggled to lift the object. With a cry of joy he pulled the treasure from the bottom of the tree trunk and held it up. Shreds of deerskin hung from the container, which was long and narrow. Gently placing the box on the ground, Brave Deer took out his hunting knife and cut away the remaining deerskin. Then, with the aid of the knife, he undid the clasps that held the box closed and lifted the lid.

'The Pipe of Peace!' gasped Susan as she looked at the long reed pipe lying undamaged in the cedar box. It was decorated with dozens of feathers of many colours, and the clay bowl was fashioned in the shape of a head.

'The head is that of Chief Wahenatha,' said Brave Deer, gently touching the pipe. 'He was the Odega chief at the time of the Council of Seven.'

'We owe this discovery to you, Susan,' said Black Cloud, admiration in his black eyes.

Suddenly Black Cloud whirled about and pulled out his knife. Brave Deer jumped to his feet, and Wolf Dog began to growl, for Mr 'Tanner' had emerged from the woods, holding Icky in his arms.

'Give me the pipe, or I will kill this cat,' he said, pointing a gun at Icky's head.

Before another second had passed, Wolf Dog sprang into the air with such speed and violence that Mr 'Tanner' shrieked and tried to run, dropping Icky to the ground. He was too slow for Wolf Dog, however, who grabbed him by the ankle with her enormous teeth.

Black Cloud and Brave Deer ran over to the man, who was struggling helplessly to free himself from Wolf Dog's grip. Black Cloud took the gun from Mr 'Tanner's' hand, and the Indian boy called off his dog. Together the two Odegas tied their captive to a tree with a stout rope that Black Cloud wore at his waist.

'You should not have tried to outwit Susan Sand,' said Black Cloud.

'Your wife is in New York trying to steal Mrs Vandervelden's necklace, isn't she, Mr "Tanner"?' Susan said.

'She will be surprised to find Barry Hearne and the New York police there to greet her.'

'We should have escaped when we had the chance,' the man murmured between clenched teeth.

'The pipe means nothing to you but money you could get for it,' said Brave Deer angrily. 'White Rabbit gave his life for it.'

Then, turning to Susan, Brave Deer thanked her for finding the Pipe of Peace. 'You have proved that White Rabbit was not a coward,' he said. 'And you have saved my uncle and me from disgrace.'

Susan accepted Brave Deer's words with a warm smile and picked up Icky.

'And thank you, Wolf Dog, for saving Icky's life,' she said. 'Let's get back to the camp and tell everyone what has happened.'

That Sunday evening there was a celebration in the private dining-room at the Feather Inn. Mrs Vandervelden was the hostess for the gala occasion and sat at the head of a long table, which was festively decorated, the Pipe of Peace prominently displayed in the centre. Claudia Kingsley, dressed in a lovely gown of pale blue, sat on Mrs Vandervelden's right, and Susan Sand on her left.

Black Cloud and Brave Deer, still wearing their buckskin jackets, sat on either side of the long table, with the Pipe of Peace directly in front of them. Mr Kingsley, beaming at his daughter, was seated next to Black Cloud, and Randall Scott, Brian, and Marge farther along the table. Barry Hearne had been placed at the other end, opposite Mrs Vandervelden, and next to him sat Rose Petal.

Wolf Dog and Ikhnaton, Amenhotep IV, were sprawled out in front of an open window, for the night was very hot, with scarcely a breeze to disturb the stillness.

Randall Scott rose to his feet, Farmer Smythe's diary in

142

his hand. 'I want to return this diary to your people, Black Cloud,' he announced. 'Irongate University feels that it should belong to the Odegas.'

'Thank you, Professor Scott,' Black Cloud replied, taking the book. 'I, in turn, will give it to Rose Petal to put on display in the museum.'

He walked to the end of the table where Rose Petal sat, and handed her the diary.

'I propose a toast,' said Barry Hearne, rising to his feet. 'To the "Tanners" for falling into the trap and for giving me the pleasure of seeing them put behind bars.'

'I would like to say one thing,' stated Susan when the laughter had died down. 'I want to praise Claudia for her bravery. By playing the "Phantom", she protected both her father and Brave Deer.'

The entire party clapped their hands in agreement and sat down to a delicious meal. Brave Deer and Claudia smiled at each other across the table, causing Susan Sand to feel both contented and sad that the adventure at Featherford Falls had drawn to a close. Soon, however, she would be involved in another mystery, when she was confronted with *The Password to Diamonddwarf Dale*.

More Beaver Books

We hope you have enjoyed this Beaver Book. Here are some of the other titles:

Super Ghosts A Beaver original. Spine-chilling accounts of hauntings in all kinds of places, from churches to pubs, houses to village greens, and featuring haunted skulls, a vampire, poltergeists and even a ghost with a bad smell! Written by Mark Ronson

The Gooseberry A realistic and amusing story about the ups and downs of Ellie Ferguson, a young Edinburgh girl, which will delight all older readers. By Joan Lingard, author of the 'Maggie' books

The Beaver Book of Horror Stories A Beaver original. A spine-chilling collection for older readers by master horror writers such as Ray Bradbury and H. P. Lovecraft; edited and with a specially written contribution by Mark Ronson

These and many other Beavers are available from your local bookshop or newsagent, or can be ordered direct from: Hamlyn Paperback Cash Sales, PO Box 11, Falmouth, Cornwall TR10 9EN. Send a cheque or postal order for the price of the book plus postage at the following rates:
UK: 45p for the first book, 20p for the second book, and 14p for each additional book ordered to a maximum charge of £1.63;
BFPO and Eire: 45p for the first book, 20p for the second book, plus 14p per copy for the next 7 books and thereafter 8p per book;
OVERSEAS: 75p for the first book and 21p for each extra book.

New Beavers are published every month and if you would like the *Beaver Bulletin*, a newsletter which tells you about new books and gives a complete list of titles and prices, send a large stamped addressed envelope to:

Beaver Bulletin
Arrow Publications
17-21 Conway Street
London W1P 6JD

936020